Paddington on Screen

"What is your special subject?" asked the quiz master of the television programme, Sage of Britain.

"Marmalade sandwiches," replied Paddington.

The Browns were very surprised at his appearance on their set. They thought they might see him in the audience, but not as a contestant sitting in the "hot seat".

But Paddington does have a tendency for surprises. Who would expect to see him on the Nine O'Clock news? Who would pay a taxi driver with used matches, and who would have to hide in the loft from Mr Curry?

The seven stories originally appeared in the Blue Peter annuals and now make up a Second Blue Peter Storybook.

OTHER YEARLING BOOKS YOU WILL ENJOY:

A BEAR CALLED PADDINGTON, *Michael Bond*
MORE ABOUT PADDINGTON, *Michael Bond*
PADDINGTON AT LARGE, *Michael Bond*
PADDINGTON AT WORK, *Michael Bond*
PADDINGTON HELPS OUT, *Michael Bond*
WITCH-CAT, *Joan Carris*
PETS, VETS, AND MARTY HOWARD, *Joan Carris*
WHEN THE BOYS RAN THE HOUSE, *Joan Carris*
RALPH S. MOUSE, *Beverly Cleary*
THE MOUSE AND THE MOTORCYCLE, *Beverly Cleary*

YEARLING BOOKS/YOUNG YEARLINGS/YEARLING CLASSICS are designed especially to entertain and enlighten young people. Charles F. Reasoner, Professor Emeritus of Children's Literature and Reading, New York University, is consultant to this series.

For a complete listing of all Yearling titles, write to Dell Readers Service, P.O. Box 1045, South Holland, IL 60473.

BY MICHAEL BOND

Paddington on Screen

Illustrated by Barry Macey

A YEARLING BOOK

Published by
Dell Publishing Co., Inc.
1 Dag Hammarskjold Plaza
New York, New York 10017

Yearling ® TM 913705, Dell Publishing Co., Inc.

ISBN: 0-440-40029-5

Reprinted by arrangement with Houghton Mifflin
Company

Printed in the United States of America

February 1988

10 9 8 7 6 5 4 3 2 1

CW

Contents

CHAPTER ONE

Paddington's Puzzle

Paddington was at a loose end. Or rather, to be more exact, he was at a loose end in the loft of number thirty-two Windsor Gardens; a situation that would have caused a certain amount of alarm among the rest of the household had they been in a position to know about it.

But fortunately for their peace of mind they were elsewhere at that moment, and busy with other things. Mr Brown was at his office; Jonathan and Judy were at school; and with Christmas only a short way away, Mrs Brown and her housekeeper,

Mrs Bird, were out for the day doing some "secret" shopping.

It was largely because he'd been left to his own devices that Paddington had eventually ended up in the loft. His own Christmas list was far from complete, and he'd really gone up there in the hope of getting some ideas from all the old things that were stored there.

Paddington was rather keen on the Browns' loft and it wasn't often he had the chance to pay it a visit. Even the act of having to climb a pair of steps and push open the trapdoor was somehow more exciting than going into an ordinary room.

It was the smell he remembered most of all; a musty mixture of moth-balls, old clothes, cardboard and dry air, that was really quite pleasant when you got used to it.

The rafters were chock-a-block with bits and pieces; boxes of long-forgotten games, old curtains, toys, rolls of carpet, dolls and packing cases overflowing with junk of every kind; in fact, there was so much he hardly knew where to start.

In the end he picked on the packing case nearest to him and began unloading it bit by bit. It was a slow job, for the more he took out the more there seemed to be left inside, and he kept coming across things that needed investigating.

He was so busy the time simply melted away, and

it was not until he came across a large cardboard
box with a brightly coloured picture on the lid that
he took his first pause for breath.

The picture showed a small boy sitting at a table,
hard at work with a most unusual looking saw, and
by a strange coincidence it was almost identical to
one John had used earlier in the week in a Blue
Peter item on fretwork. Seeing the picture brought
it all back and set Paddington's mind awhirl.

Paddington liked carpentry, but he did not get
much opportunity to do any. Whenever Mrs Bird
saw him with tools in his paws she always sent him
out into the garden, and the idea of having a carpentry set you were actually *meant* to use indoors
seemed a very good idea indeed.

The inside of the box was even more exciting, for it was still full of the original tools — each one mounted in its own specially shaped hole. Admittedly the fretsaw had gone slightly rusty over the years, but there were several unused blades left, not to mention a small drill, some sandpaper, several sheets of plywood, and a selection of paper patterns for good measure.

Paddington came to a decision. His find seemed like a heaven-sent opportunity to kill several birds with one stone. He felt sure that even Mrs Bird couldn't be cross with him if he used the outfit in order to make some Christmas presents for the rest of the family, and a few moments later, clutching the box in his paws, he clambered back through the trapdoor and hurried downstairs.

His first port of call was the kitchen, and for the next half hour all was quiet as he busied himself making up some flour and water paste so that he could stick the various patterns on to the plywood, just as John had shown on the television.

Paddington did not believe in doing things by halves, and he soon had a bucket overflowing with the paste ready for the off.

Shortly afterwards, back in his own room, a steady sound of sawing filled the air as he set to work.

At first sight, even though they'd been well and

truly stuck to the plywood, the patterns looked a bit complicated. But remembering some of the tips John had passed on, about always keeping the wood firm and level and the fretsaw itself upright so that the blade didn't twist and break, everything seemed to go surprisingly well. The nice thing about fretwork seemed to be that you never, ever, followed a straight line when a wiggly one would do, and this suited Paddington down to the ground, because some of his own lines were very wiggly indeed.

The more he did the more pleased he began to feel about the way things were going. In no time at all he'd completed quite a number of items — more even than were shown on the lid of the box. Mr Brown had come off best of all, with no less than three pipe racks; but there were also a trinket box for Mrs Brown, a saucepan-lid holder for Mrs Bird, a tie-rack for Jonathan, and another smaller box for Judy to keep her odds and ends in.

Unfortunately, when he blew the sawdust away he found he'd also made a hole in the top of his dressing table.

Paddington was most upset about the hole, but luckily he managed to find the missing piece, and after busying himself with a pot of glue he soon had it almost back to normal. In fact, after rubbing the spot with some marmalade it was hard to see where it had happened.

It was while he was mending the hole in his dressing table that Paddington suddenly had an idea for what was really one of his most important Christmas presents of all; the one he always sent to the Blue Peter team.

It was never easy trying to think up presents for all four, and although Paddington was a generous bear at heart, he somehow felt it was much better value to send one good one they could all share rather than several not such good ones.

Until it had been repaired, the top of his dressing table had looked not unlike an unfinished jig-saw puzzle, and a jig-saw puzzle seemed the ideal answer to his problem. Paddington was sure that given the right picture he would be able to make a very good puzzle indeed.

Many times in the past he'd found that ideas and good luck often went together — the one seemingly being triggered off by the other, and it was while he was gazing out of his window wondering where on earth he could find a suitable picture, that the kitchen door belonging to the house next door suddenly opened and Mr Curry, the Browns' neighbour, came into view carrying a large, oblong object in his arms.

Even as far away as his bedroom window Paddington could see that it was a picture of some kind, and his eyes grew larger and larger as Mr Curry, after hesitating for a moment or two, propped it against his dustbin and then went back into his house.

Paddington could hardly believe his good fortune. Normally he wouldn't have dreamed of asking the Browns' neighbour for anything. Apart from having a reputation for being extremely bad-tempered, Mr Curry was also well-known in the district for his meanness. He rarely, if ever, threw things away, so if he put anything out with the rubbish it was a certainty he couldn't possibly have any further use for it.

Paddington hurried downstairs and made his way round the side of the house. In order to make doubly sure he knocked on Mr Curry's back door, but there was such a noise going on inside the house even though he tried several times there was no reply, so he turned his attention to the matter in hand.

The picture wasn't the only thing Mr Curry had put out with his rubbish. Standing beside the dustbin was a pile of old magazines, an occasional table, an umbrella stand, and various other items.

Paddington recognized the picture as one Mr Curry usually kept hanging in his hall. It showed a gentleman in frilly clothes and a feathered hat. He wore a large moustache and a happy smile on his face, but what pleased Paddington most of all was the fact that he was already stuck to a sheet of plywood — just right for cutting.

Paddington considered the matter for a moment or two. All in all, he decided that perhaps it would be better not to bother Mr Curry again in case it made him change his mind. Apart from that, he was anxious to begin work on the jig-saw, and so, after tapping lightly once more on the door, he picked up the painting and made his way back home without waiting to see if the knocks were answered.

Paddington soon decided that cutting out jig-saw puzzles was much the best use for a fretsaw. It was even easier than making pipe-racks. It was really only a matter of moving the saw up and down as fast as it would go, turning the wood in different directions at the same time, and he grew more and more pleased as one by one the pieces fell to the floor and the pile at his feet grew higher.

When he got to the end he put them all carefully into a cardboard box, wrapped the box itself in some special Christmas paper, and then spent some time making out a label marked A PRESENT FOR YOU in large green letters.

As it happened the ink had barely time to dry when there was a ring at the front door bell, and thinking perhaps the Browns had arrived home extra early Paddington hurried downstairs with the parcel.

To his surprise it wasn't the Browns at all; it was Mr Curry. He didn't seem in a very good mood, and for some reason or other he sounded even more cross when Paddington announced that he was on his own.

"I'd like to use your 'phone, bear," he growled, as he followed Paddington into the hall. "I have just been robbed of a very valuable item. And I might say it isn't surprising if everybody goes out. It's asking for trouble."

While he was talking, Mr Curry caught sight of the box in Paddington's paws, and when he saw the words on the lid his expression softened.

"Fancy you going to all that trouble just for me, bear!" he exclaimed, all thoughts of his telephone call forgotten for the moment.

Paddington stared at him in alarm. "Oh, I haven't been to any trouble for *you*, Mr Curry," he began. "I *wouldn't* ... I mean..."

Mr Curry held up his hand. "There's no need to say another word, bear," he announced, pushing open the dining-room door. "I shan't wait until Christmas. I shall open it here and now."

Paddington watched gloomily as without further ado Mr Curry tore open the paper and emptied the contents of the box on to the table. Although he always sent the Browns' neighbour a card he didn't normally give him any sort of a present, let alone one he'd made specially for the Blue Peter team.

"I'm afraid it's only a jig-saw, Mr Curry," he explained. "I made it with my own paws. If you like," he added hopefully, "I could try and do you something better."

'Nonsense, bear!" said Mr Curry, in an un-usually mild tone of voice. "I like jig-saws. I don't know when anyone last gave me one. I must say I'm very touched."

Mr Curry seemed so taken up with the whole affair he began sorting out the pieces straight away. "This is just what I need," he explained. "Something to take my mind off things.

"I've been redecorating my hall," he continued, "and I know you won't believe this, but I stood all the things outside while I was working and someone has stolen a very valuable painting. I left it propped against the dustbin. It could only have been there a few minutes."

Paddington's face grew longer and longer as he listened to Mr Curry.

"I *do* believe you, Mr Curry," he said unhappily as he hurried across the room and began drawing the curtains.

Mr Curry stared after him. "Bear!" he roared, some of his usual bad temper getting the better of him. "What are you doing? I can't see to do my jigsaw!"

"That's good!" exclaimed Paddington. "I ... I mean ..." He broke off as he caught sight of the expression on Mr Curry's face, and he began juggling with the folds in the material in the hope of finding a position where the gap let in enough light for the shape of the pieces to be visible without giving away the whole picture.

"My painting," said Mr Curry, placing another piece of puzzle carefully into its correct position, "has been in the family for as long as I can remember. I would go so far as to say it's priceless! Funnily enough, it wasn't unlike ..."

The Browns' neighbour gave a start as he stared

at the half-completed puzzle in front of him.

"Bear!" he bellowed suddenly. "What's the meaning of this? Where are you? Come back here!"

But Mr Curry's words fell on stony ground, for Paddington had fled. He felt the moment had definitely come to make himself scarce, and he knew just the place in which to do it.

Although in the course of the day he'd removed quite a few things from the Browns' loft it was still pretty full, and there was certainly more than enough left to make a very good cover for a bear's hideaway.

Paddington felt pleased he'd picked such a good hiding-place. Mr Curry stomped around the house calling out his name for some while, and when he risked a quick peep through the trapdoor it gave him quite a shock; for anything less like the happy, smiling face of the man in the jig-saw picture would have been hard to imagine.

But at long last there was a bang and the house shook as the front door slammed shut.

Just to be on the safe side Paddington sat where he was for a moment or two until he felt the coast was clear, and then he crept downstairs. Once there, he made his way in the direction of the telephone, for with Mr Curry in his present mood he had no wish to venture outside. There was no need to look up the number he had in mind, for he'd had occasion to dial it more than once in the past.

Paddington was a great believer in going straight to the top in times of trouble, and he felt sure that if the members of the Blue Peter team put their heads together they would be able to think of a way out of his present emergency, especially as it had to do with fretwork and their own Christmas present into the bargain.

John gave a cough. "One of the nice things about working on Blue Peter," he said, addressing the viewing millions, "is that life is full of surprises."

"Never a dull moment," agreed Peter.

"Who would have thought," continued Lesley, with a straight face, "that when we came into the studio this morning we would end up being the proud owners of a bear's restoration!"

"What's that?" bellowed Mr Curry. He peered

at the Browns' television screen as the camera pulled back to reveal an all-too-familiar picture. "That's *my* painting! What's it doing on Blue Peter? Bear! Is this anything to do with you?"

Mr Curry glared round the Browns' dining-room, but if he was hoping for an answer he was disappointed. Paddington was keeping well out of sight, hidden from view by the rest of the family.

The Browns themselves were equally at sea. They had arrived back from their shopping expedition only to find Mr Curry standing on their front doorstep clutching a telegram bearing the words "IF YOU WATCH BLUE PETER THIS AFTERNOON YOU MAY SEE SOMETHING TO YOUR ADVANTAGE. VAL. LESLEY. JOHN AND PETER." But beyond that they had no knowledge of what had been going on that day. Only Mrs Bird had a nasty feeling it might have something to do with Paddington, and Mr Curry's latest outburst confirmed her worst suspicions.

"If you sit still and listen for a moment," she said severely, "perhaps we shall *all* find out what's going on!"

"This painting," said John, as Mr Curry sank back muttering into his chair, "came into our hands just before the programme went on the air."

"You might think," said Peter, running his

fingers over the surface, "that it's a priceless work of art."

"Hear! Hear!" murmured Mr Curry, glancing triumphantly at the others. "I'm glad someone's talking sense at last."

"If you thought that," said Lesley, "you would be quite wrong. It's a copy of a very famous painting called The Laughing Cavalier, and it's certainly priceless in one meaning of the word — you can practically buy them two a penny."

"Oh, I wouldn't say that," broke in John. "*Three* a penny is more like it. You see them all over the place. In fact, just to prove it we went out and bought some more."

While he was speaking the camera pulled back still further and Valerie came into view standing beside a whole row of identical paintings. She crossed towards Mr Curry's painting and with a single deft movement placed it on a nearby table, removing it from the frame at the same time.

"What makes this one different to the others," she said, "is that it's really two-in-one. You can either have it hanging up ..."

"Or," said John, as he joined her and broke off one of the corners and held it up to the camera, "you can use it as a jig-saw."

"Just the thing for the long winter evenings," broke in Lesley.

"But what makes it even more interesting," said Peter, as a closer shot of Mr Curry's painting filled the screen, "is that when it's used as a picture it looks exactly like the real thing. The saw-cuts are just like the sort of cracks you get in the paint on a genuine old master."

"In fact," said Valerie, "we're so pleased with our present we are going to hang it in a place of honour in the Blue Peter office. And so that its original owner won't feel too deprived we're sending him one of the other paintings."

"In a spanking new frame," said John. "Which in itself," he added meaningly, "is worth more than the old one *and* its picture put together."

"So we hope everyone will be happy," concluded Peter. "*We* certainly are. We have a new picture for the office ..."

"Plus the fun of doing a jig-saw," added Lesley.

"The taxi-driver got an unexpected fare when I went to collect it," continued John.

"The Producers had an item for today's programme," said Valerie, "and last but not least, I expect a good many viewers will have got some ideas for their own Christmas presents as well."

"Perhaps, Mr Curry," said Paddington hopefully, as he emerged from behind the sofa, "when your new painting comes I could turn that into a jig-saw as well!"

But his offer fell on deaf ears. The Browns' neighbour was already on his way. And if the expression on his face was anything to go by, the answer to Paddington's offer was most definitely "no". Mr Curry looked as if he'd had quite enough of bears' jig-saw puzzles for the time being.

As it was, he missed John's closing remark after he'd announced that they would be sending the remaining paintings to Paddington that very afternoon. It was a remark that caused a loud groan to go up not only from Peter, Val and Lesley, but the Browns as well, and one which, had he still been there, Mr Curry would have agreed with to the full.

"After all," said John, "Paddington might want to do some more fretwork and I'd hate to think of him going next-door for another picture. *That* would be the unkindest saw-cut of all!"

CHAPTER TWO

A Spoonful of Paddington

Dipping his paw into a bowl of rather gritty orange-coloured liquid standing on a table beside his bed, Paddington shook off some loose drips which had stuck to his fur, and picked up a small silvery object lying nearby.

Giving it a hard stare, he rubbed it vigorously for several minutes and then, as his whiskers started to sag under the strain, he held it up to the light and surveyed the result of his labours before turning his attention to a large sheet of squared paper spread out across the bed.

Running his paw down a column on the left hand edge, he stopped at a vacant spot, exchanged the object for a felt pen, and carefully wrote in the words: EGGSPERRYMENT NUMBER FOURTY-SEVEN — MARMALADE AND BAYKING POWDER MICKSTURE.

After a moment's thought he gloomily added the word *FAYLED* and was about to underline it several more times for good measure, when he happened to glance up. The whole operation had taken rather longer than he'd expected, and catching sight of the time he dropped the pen and hastily donned his duffle-coat and hat. Shortly afterwards, having been into the kitchen in order to say goodbye to the rest of the family, he disappeared out through the front door as fast as his legs would carry him.

Paddington wasn't the sort of bear to remain down in the dumps for long, even when things weren't going his way, but all the same he wore a very disappointed look on his face indeed as he hurried down the road in the direction of the market.

But Paddington wasn't the only member of the Brown household to be unhappy about the result of his afternoon's work. The front door had hardly closed behind him when Mr Brown put down a tea towel he'd been using and held up a badly bent spoon for everyone to see.

"What on earth's happened to this?" he exclaimed. "Just look at the state it's in. Anyone would think it had been put through the mangle backwards."

"Oh dear!" Mrs Brown looked up anxiously from her sink. "That's the third one today." She felt in the soapy water. "And here's another one. It's a good thing they're not part of our best set."

"If you ask me," said Mrs Bird, their housekeeper, "it's got something to do with that television programme we saw the other evening. The one everybody's talking about. That one with Uri Geller. I've heard lots of strange tales ever since. People's watches stopping for no reason at all, and goodness knows what else."

Jonathan and Judy exchanged glances. "I think," said Judy, "it's probably got rather more to do with Paddington."

"He's got a touch of the Uri Gellers himself," agreed Jonathan.

"He didn't have much luck reading our secret messages," continued Judy, "so he's been trying spoon-bending instead. Only it's a bit difficult with paws. He keeps on bending the handles by mistake ..." Her voice trailed away as she caught sight of the look on her father's face.

"You must admit, Henry," said Mrs Brown, pouring oil on troubled waters, "that you were quite keen on it yourself at the time. I saw you having a quiet go with the coffee-spoons afterwards."

Mr Brown fell silent. He had to agree that like most people he'd fallen under the spell of Uri Geller, and that like most people he'd also joined in the general argument afterwards as to whether his many feats, performed under the close scrutiny of the television cameras and millions of viewers, were the result of simple, but brilliantly performed magic, or some kind of supernatural powers beyond anyone's understanding.

"Being keen is one thing," he said at last. "Bending all the cutlery is another. We shan't have any left at this rate." He held the spoon under the hot tap. "What on earth's he been putting on them . . . glue?"

"I expect it's one of his special mixtures," said Jonathan. "I think he read that someone had a theory about chemicals being used."

"*Chemicals!*" Mrs Bird gave a snort. "There are more things in heaven and earth than we've ever dreamed of," she said darkly. "Some people won't believe the evidence of their own eyes."

"I don't know about Paddington having a touch of the Uri Gellers," said Mr Brown, wiping his hands on a towel. "It feels more like the Uri Gagas to me." He gave the offending item a closer inspection. "Marmalade!" he exclaimed in disgust. "Dried marmalade! No wonder that bear was in a hurry to leave."

If Mr Brown had been able to share some of Uri Geller's special powers at that moment Paddington might well have reappeared at number thirty-two Windsor Gardens rather quicker than he'd left. But in saying he'd gone out in a hurry solely because of the state of the cutlery, Mr Brown was, for once, doing him an injustice.

As it happened, Paddington had several very good reasons for being in a hurry.

To start with, there was less than an hour to go before Blue Peter was on the air. Paddington rarely missed a Blue Peter programme, and the one that day promised to be even more interesting than usual, for it had been announced that as a follow-up to Uri Geller's recent appearance, viewers with similar experiences in other parts of the country had been invited to the studios to take part.

But the main reason for Paddington's haste was the fact that earlier in the day he'd received an unexpected, but obviously urgent invitation to join his friend, Mr Gruber, for tea.

Mr Gruber kept an antique shop in the Portobello Road. Paddington often called in for his elevenses in the mornings, but apart from occasional outings, it was very rare for them to have tea

together, and he was looking forward to it.

Mr Gruber already had the crockery laid out on a small table at the back of his shop when Paddington arrived. He seemed to have something on his mind, but it wasn't until they had settled themselves on the horse-hair sofa reserved for such occasions that he actually got down to the subject in hand.

Clearing his throat, he glanced at Paddington over the top of his glasses. "Er, Mr Brown," he said. "I've been wondering if you would be kind enough to do me a favour?

"A young niece of mine arrived unexpectedly today, and I've promised to take her round London this evening and show her some of the sights. The trouble is," and here Mr Gruber began to look even more embarrassed, "she's brought my little grand-nephew, Ambrose, with her. We can't very well take him with us, and we've no-one to leave him with . . . so I was wondering if you could possibly babysit for us?"

Paddington nearly dropped his cup of tea with surprise. Over the years Mr Gruber had done many things for him, and he was only too pleased to have the chance of doing something in return.

"It's very kind of you," said Mr Gruber. "I shall rest easy in my mind now. We shall be going along Windsor Gardens — I want to show my niece where you live, so I can call in and tell Mr and Mrs Brown where you are. But I thought I would ask you first. I wouldn't want you to think I was going over your head."

Having settled the matter, Mr Gruber cleared away the tea things and led the way upstairs.

Mr Gruber's niece looked at Paddington rather doubtfully as they were introduced. There was still some marmalade mixture left on his whiskers, and she couldn't help but notice that his paw was defin-itely sticky to the touch.

"Have you had much experience?" she enquired dubiously.

"Well," said Paddington, raising his hat politely with his other paw. "Yes, and no."

30

"Mr Brown is a very experienced bear," said Mr Gruber hurriedly. "And *very* reliable."

Mr Gruber went on to relate some of Paddington's past adventures, and his niece began to look slightly more impressed. She hadn't met many bears before and one couldn't always go by appearances.

"Well, I hope Ambrose is good," she said. "He's just reached the stage when he's into everything, so I'll leave him in his pram just to be on the safe side."

Mr Gruber picked up a cardboard box. "I've collected some odds and ends from the shop," he announced, emptying the contents on to the flat canopy of the pram. "They should keep him amused."

"I've put some food out," broke in his niece. "It's all ready, so there's no need to do any cooking."

"And if you do get stuck," added Mr Gruber, as they made ready to leave, "you'll find a book of instructions on the table."

Paddington felt most important as he leaned out of the upstairs window and waved goodbye to the others. He'd never actually been left in charge of anyone before, and what with that and the thought of the Blue Peter programme to come, he was very much looking forward to his evening.

But his pleasure was short-lived, for just as he was giving a final wave something sharp and heavy hit him on the back of his head. He looked round just in time to see one of Mr Gruber's odds and ends, in the shape of a toy building brick, roll under the table.

Paddington gave the occupant of the pram one of his hardest ever stares. Almost immediately he had cause to regret his action, for an ear-splitting howl rent the air. It sounded like a mixture of a faulty ambulance siren and someone undergoing some kind of severe and unmentionable torture. But what was even worse was the fact that it showed no sign whatsoever of stopping.

It was so loud and piercing it caused a number of passers-by in the street outside to stop and look up in alarm.

Closing the window, Paddington hopefully consulted Mr Gruber's instruction book. But as he turned the pages his face began to fall. It was a large and rather rambling book, and it had obviously been written in a more leisurely age for those who not only had a lot of time on their hands, but who also owned a very different baby to Ambrose. In fact, the one they had used in the illustrations looked as unlike Ambrose as chalk from cheese. Whereas the one in the book seemed to spend most of its life lying on its back with its legs in the air, gurgling happily as the author whispered sweet nothings into its ear, Ambrose was sitting bolt upright, and was clearly all set to yell his head off for the rest of the evening. Not even the sweetest of nothings seemed likely to divert him from his aim, and the only good thing about the situation was the knowledge that he was firmly strapped into his pram, otherwise there was no knowing what might have happened.

Paddington glanced anxiously at Mr Gruber's clock. Come what may, he was determined to watch the Blue Peter programme, but with the hands coming up to ten minutes to five matters were beginning to get a trifle desperate.

Paddington was a great believer in food during times of trouble, and having switched the television set on to warm up, he emptied the contents of a tin of strained apple into a bowl, mixed in an extra-large dollop of marmalade for good measure, and grabbed a spoon from a small pile on the canopy of the pram.

He was only just in time, for no sooner had he placed the bowl on Ambrose's lap than the familiar strains of the Blue Peter signature tune started up and the opening picture appeared on the screen.

To his relief the diversion seemed to have an almost magical effect on Ambrose, for he fell silent almost at once. Feeling rather more pleased with himself, Paddington grabbed a nearby stool and settled down to watch the programme.

It began with a preview of the spoon-bending item to come. John, Peter and Lesley were shown seated amongst a group of other participants. They were all busily rubbing away at various shapes and sizes of spoons, and if the sighs and grunts were anything to go by, they were no nearer success than Paddington had been earlier in the day. In fact, he was just beginning to wish he'd brought some of his own spoons along so that he could join in, too, when he heard a commotion going on behind him.

" 'poon!" cried Ambrose. " 'poon! 'poon!"

Paddington glanced round and then nearly fell backwards off his stool with surprise. The cause of his astonishment wasn't the sight of Ambrose beaming at him through a thick layer of strained apple and marmalade; it was the object he was clutching in his hand.

Imitating the people on the television screen, he was rubbing his spoon with his other hand and, even as Paddington watched, it began to bend in the middle until the business end was almost at right angles to the handle itself.

But there was an even bigger surprise to come. Torn between watching Blue Peter and keeping an eye on Ambrose, Paddington stole a quick look at the screen again. When he turned back, Ambrose had discarded the first spoon and was now hard at work doing exactly the same thing to a second one.

Paddington rubbed his eyes in order to make sure he wasn't dreaming, and in the short time they were closed yet another bent spoon added itself to the pile in the pram. From the gurgles of delight which rose from Ambrose it was clear that the baby who'd played such a leading part in Mr Gruber's book would need to look to its laurels if it ever came up against him in a "Happiest Child of the Year" contest.

Paddington came to a decision. Mr Gruber's shop was within walking distance of the BBC Television Studios, and with nearly twenty minutes of the programme still left he was certain he could make it in time.

The Blue Peter team had said they were anxious to hear from viewers with unusual experiences of spoon-bending, and Paddington felt sure they would be more than interested in Ambrose's efforts. Not even Mr Geller at his peak had ever managed to bend his spoons at quite such a rate.

If the inhabitants of West London felt any surprise at seeing a pram hurtle past, propelled by a small figure in a blue duffle-coat, they showed no sign. Or if they did, Paddington was going much too fast to notice.

He hardly stopped running until he reached the

Television Centre, where he found his progress
barred by a burly commissionaire.

"You can't bring that pram in here," said the
man sternly. "For all I know you might have a
bomb hidden inside."

" 'poon! 'poon!" cried Ambrose. And waving his
latest effort in the air, he gave vent to his most
piercing yell to date.

The commissionaire shifted uneasily as Paddington launched into a hurried explanation of why he
was there. It all sounded highly unlikely, but as he
peered inside the pram and saw all the bent spoons
his expression changed.

"Sounds more like a bomb*shell* to me," said a second commissionaire. He held up his hands to his ears as Ambrose's yells grew even louder at the sight of all the faces. "I should let them in if I were you."

There was a flurry of movement from the cameras and microphone booms as Paddington and Ambrose were ushered into the Blue Peter studio. The programme was drawing to a close, but even so the technicians rapidly took up fresh positions so that they could cover the situation.

It was a movement which was more than echoed at number thirty-two Windsor Gardens as everyone crowded round the television receiver.

"Ambrose!" cried Mr Gruber's niece.

"Paddington!" gasped the others.

"What on earth's he up to now?" exclaimed Mr Brown.

"Oh, gosh!" groaned Judy, as a close-up shot of a spoon appeared on the screen. "Don't say he's at it again!"

It was hard to tell who was the most surprised — Mr Gruber and his niece, who hadn't long left Paddington and Ambrose; or the Browns, who had only just been told what Paddington was supposed to be doing. They all watched in silent fascination as the camera zoomed out slowly to reveal Ambrose hard at work on his spoon-bending act. He seemed

to be enjoying the fact that he was the centre of so much attention, and a moment later John, Peter and Lesley came into view as they crowded round to offer their congratulations.

"I've heard of people getting the bends," said John admiringly, "but this is ridiculous."

"It's phenomonal," agreed Peter and Lesley.

"It's stewed apple and marmalade," said Paddington.

"It's a fake!" exclaimed Mr Gruber.

To everyone's astonishment he jumped to his feet and rushed towards the door. "I think perhaps I'd better make a quick telephone call," he announced. "I'm afraid young Mr Brown's a victim of one of my joke spoons!"

Mr Gruber stood in the middle of the deserted Blue Peter studio and held up a spoon. He rubbed it gently near the middle, and there was a round of applause as it slowly bent in two.

"I'm afraid it's part of a job lot I bought the other day," he said rather sheepishly. "It isn't one of my normal lines, but after that television programme the other evening I got the feeling that quite a lot of people might be wanting to fool their friends and pretend they could do the same thing as Uri Geller. But unlike Mr Geller's spoons this one has a hinge in the middle."

"I told you there are more things in heaven and earth than we've ever dreamed of," said Mrs Bird.

"I don't think I've ever dreamed of a spoon with hinges," said Paddington in amazement.

"You nearly fooled seven million viewers," said Lesley.

"Not to mention all of us," chuckled John. "It's a good job your telephone call came through when it did. Otherwise our switchboard would have been swamped."

Mr Gruber nodded. "On the other hand," he said, "you can fool all the people some of the time, and some of the people all the time ..."

"But you can't fool all the people all the time," agreed Peter. "The truth will always come out in the end."

John gazed at the spoon in Ambrose's hand, and then at the remains of his apple and marmalade. "All of which," he said, rubbing his stomach, "makes me feel hungry. I vote that after we've shown Mr Gruber's niece round the studios we all go out for a meal in a Chinese restaurant."

"A *Chinese restaurant?*" Among the cries of surprise which greeted this remark, Paddington's voice was by far the loudest. All the same, he licked his lips in anticipation, for it sounded a very good way indeed of rounding things off.

"Chinese restaurants," said John with a straight face, "have chopsticks. I don't suppose even Uri Geller himself could do anything with those."

"Glug!" gurgled Ambrose happily as he handed Paddington the last of the spoons. "Glug! Glug! ... 'poon! 'poon! Glug!"

"And you can't," said John, amid general agreement, "say any fairer than that!"

CHAPTER THREE

Paddington Clocks In

Paddington gazed at the Browns' television set as if he could hardly believe his eyes.

"My horse came in at ten to one!" he exclaimed. "But it left at half past twelve!"

The rest of the family exchanged anxious glances. "It doesn't mean your horse took twenty minutes to run the race," explained Mrs Brown. "It's all to do with the odds. Ten to one means you get back ten times the amount you put on."

"Which means I've won thirty matches," said Jonathan. "I bet three matches that *Marmalade*

41

would win and he has."

"You should have stuck to it yourself," broke in Judy.

"He usually does," said Jonathan, trying to make light of the whole affair. "Marmalade, I mean ... er ... that is ..."

But their words were falling on deaf ears. Paddington's attention was still rivetted to the television screen.

Until the last race the Browns had been enjoying a quiet game of "Spot the Winner". Armed with a list of runners from the daily paper, they had been watching the horse-racing at Sandown Park, adding a little spice to the proceedings by taking matchsticks from a pile on the table and placing bets on the various events.

Paddington himself had made a very good start to the day, mostly by working on a system of backing horses whose names he fancied. After two winners in succession — *Portobello Road* in the first race and *Plum Cake* in the second, his pile of used matches had grown quite large, and when they looked up the third race and discovered there was a horse called *Marmalade* running he seemed all set to sweep the board with a hat trick.

But just before the start, Desmond O'Donnelly, the famous BBC Racing Commentator, had let fall a piece of inside information about one of the other runners. It was, he'd said, a tip straight from the horse's mouth, and one so hot he was putting his shirt on the result; a fact which caused Paddington to waver at the last moment and change his bet.

In the event Mr O'Donnelly had not only got his facts wrong, but he also seemed to have gone back on what he'd said he would do. Far from losing a shirt, he appeared to be taking particular pride in displaying his own in all its glory as he beamed over the top of his field-glasses at those viewers who were lucky enough to possess a colour receiver.

But it was the simple matter of getting the time wrong that upset Paddington most of all. Even he could see that it was still nowhere near twenty minutes to one, let alone ten to. If hard stares could have been transmitted back through the system to the cameras at Sandown Park, then Desmond O'Donnelly would have dropped his microphone and disappeared down the course faster than any of the horses he was at present trying his hardest to describe.

Paddington came to a decision. "I think," he announced, gathering up what was left of his winnings, "I would like to be excused."

"Oh dear," said Mrs Brown as the door closed behind him, "he does seem to be taking it rather badly. I hope it doesn't put him off his lunch."

"It'll take more than a few lost matchsticks to

put that bear off his food," said Mrs Bird. "I'll wager the rest of my matches he'll have got over it before the next lot of horses are under starter's orders."

The Browns' housekeeper knew Paddington's eating habits of old, and it was rare indeed for him to miss a meal, so with that comforting thought in mind she turned her attention back to the television screen.

It was lucky for Paddington that she did, for had Mrs Bird not been concentrating on the commentary her sharp ears might well have caught some ominous rummaging noises going on in one of the upstairs cupboards. They were followed by several short bursts of muffled tinkling, and a moment or so later by the sound of the front door latch clicking shut; but by then the next race was well under way and everyone was much too excited to notice.

Paddington heaved a sigh of relief when he found himself safely outside number thirty-two Windsor Gardens. He was a bear with a strong sense of right and wrong, but he knew from past experience that he couldn't always count on one hundred per cent support in his campaigns for justice, and he had a feeling that if the rest of the family knew where he was going this might be one of those occasions.

Luckily, no sooner had he closed the front door than a taxi came into view. Paddington didn't normally travel by taxi, but there was no time to be lost, so he decided to jump in and worry about paying for the fare out of his bun reserves later.

"I'd like to go to the BBC Television Centre, please," he announced, as the driver held the back door open for him. "I want to get there before the last race if I can."

"Righto, mate!" As he slipped the cab into gear, the driver glanced round and caught sight of Paddington's suitcase. "You can pay me out of your winnings, if you like," he chuckled.

Paddington looked most surprised at his unexpected piece of good fortune. "Thank you very much!" he exclaimed. "Mind you," he added doubtfully, "I haven't got very many left after the last race."

"I know the feeling," said the driver sympathetically. "It happens to the best of us."

Glad of an audience, the driver started up a running commentary on the hazards of gambling in general and backing horses in particular. It lasted for most of the journey; in fact, he talked so much that Paddington was barely halfway through the marmalade sandwich he'd brought to while away the time when they reached their destination.

Paddington was a well-known figure at the Television Centre. He'd been there a number of times in the past in order to visit the Blue Peter studios, and as it was a Thursday the commissionaire on duty assumed it was another such occasion. As soon as he caught sight of the familiar blue duffle-coat in the back of the taxi he gave a cheery nod, lifted the barrier, and waved them on their way.

Paddington raised his hat politely as they drew to a halt outside the glass door of the entrance hall. "I shan't be very long," he announced. "But I've got to make sure I get the right person first. I want the man in charge of horse racing," he added impressively.

Opening his suitcase, he put the remains of the marmalade sandwich carefully away, made some last-minute adjustments to something else, and then leaned forward and peered through the sliding glass panel behind the driver's head. "I've got a

surprise for him," he whispered into the man's ear.
"It's due to go off in about five minutes!"

As he climbed out of the cab Paddington felt
inside his duffle-coat pocket. "These are my winnings," he explained, pressing his paw into the
man's hand. "If you look after my suitcase for me
while I'm gone you can keep the change as well."

The driver was too busy wiping the marmalade
from his ear to notice straight away what he'd been
given, but when he did open his hand he gazed at
it in astonishment. "'ere!" he cried. "What's all
this?"

But Paddington had already disappeared from
view somewhere inside the vast building.

"Anything the matter?" asked one of the commissionaires, as he strolled across and caught sight
of the look on the driver's face.

"Anything the matter?" repeated the driver bit-
terly. "I'll say there is. Look!" And he held out
some objects in his hand for the other to see.

"That's what's the matter ... I've just been paid
in matches ... *used* ones at that! Wait 'till I catch
'im!"

He glanced round his cab and as he did so his
gaze alighted on the back seat. A strange look suddenly came over his face. "I'll tell you something
else," he cried in alarm, as he jumped out. "I reckon
we'd best be getting out of 'ere. If you ask me

there's not a moment to be lost!"

Unaware of the drama going on five floors below, the man in charge of Racing Programmes looked impatiently at his secretary. "I really can't have people coming in here to see me unannounced like this," he complained.

"Well, it isn't exactly a *person*," said his secretary uneasily. "And he wouldn't take no for an answer. He said it was very urgent and it has to do with today's racing."

"All right," said her boss wearily. "Show him in." He sometimes wished television programmes didn't have such things as viewers. You could please most of them a good deal of the time, but there was no pleasing everybody all the time.

"I.C.R.P. will see you now," said his secretary, as she ushered Paddington into the room.

"Good afternoon, Mr Arpy," said Paddington, holding out his paw as he advanced across the room. "I'm sorry you're icy. You can borrow my duffle-coat if you like. I'm really quite warm."

The man behind the desk gave Paddington a bemused look. "I really don't quite understand," he began.

"You're lucky I've got it with me," continued Paddington. "I nearly lost it just now."

"You nearly lost your duffle-coat?" repeated the man in charge of racing. "Have you complained to the cloakroom?"

Paddington ignored the remark. "Mr O'Donnelly told me to put my shirt on a horse," he explained patiently. "But bears don't wear shirts, so it could have been my duffle-coat instead."

The man's face cleared slightly. "Do you mean to say you're complaining about one of Desmond O'Donnelly's forecasts?" he asked.

"Yes," said Paddington, glad he'd got his point over at last. "I put my matchsticks on an also-ran and it came in last."

"Well, I'm sorry you're not happy," said the man in charge of racing. "All our commentators are very experienced, but they really can't guarantee a winner every time. Mr O'Donnelly himself has been in the field for a number of years."

"Perhaps that's why he made a mistake with the time," broke in Paddington. "I expect his watch has got damp.

"He said it was ten to one," he continued, warming to his subject, "and it was really only just gone half past twelve. But don't worry, I've brought him a present. It's outside in a taxi."

The I.C.R.P. passed a trembling hand across his brow. He had a strange ringing noise in his head. He wasn't sure if it had to do with his visitor or not, but whatever the reason he wished it would go away.

Before he had a chance to say anything more the door burst open and his secretary rushed into the room. "Quick!" she cried. "The emergency bells are going. Somebody's planted a bomb outside and they're evacuating the building. It's ticking away like mad and they've sent for the disposal squad. Whoever left it said it's due to go off in five minutes!"

Paddington followed the others across to the window, and as he peered through the glass he nearly fell over backwards with astonishment.

The circular forecourt, which a few minutes before had been alive with people as they hurried to and fro about their work, was now deserted. The taxi he'd arrived in was now some distance away, and beyond that again crowds of sightseers were being held back by a bevy of commissionaires who were forming a makeshift barrier.

However, it wasn't all this activity that caused Paddington's alarm; it was the sight of an object surrounded by sandbags just outside the front doors. Even from the fifth floor he was able to recognize it immediately.

"That's not a bomb they're disposing of!" he exclaimed hotly. "That's my suitcase!"

If the entire Television Centre had suddenly vanished into thin air the watching spectators could hardly have been more surprised than they were

when Paddington suddenly emerged from the
building and hurried across the forecourt with a
determined expression on his face.

A hush fell over everyone as he clambered over
the top of the sandbags; a hush that was only equalled
by the cheer which went up a moment or so later
when he reappeared clutching the suitcase. Holding
it up for all to see, he started to unload it.

"Blimey!" said a voice in the crowd, as Paddington picked up a white object and placed it in his
mouth. "I've never seen anything like this before.
I reckon 'e deserves a medal."

"Hear! Hear!" agreed someone else. "The
M.B.E. at least."

"More like the D.C.M. if you ask me," murmured John Noakes as he and the rest of the Blue Peter team joined in the general rush to congratulate Paddington. *"Don't Come Monday!* That's the first time I've ever seen anyone defuse a marmalade sandwich!"

"What's he holding up?" gasped Lesley as they drew near. "It looks like an alarm clock."

"It *is* an alarm clock, Miss Judd," said Paddington, pleased to see a familiar face at long last. He shook the object in his paw and then held it up to his ear. "Only I don't think it's working any more," he added sadly. "It must have stopped ticking when I picked it up.

"It was really meant to be a present for Mr O'Donnelly," he explained. "He's having trouble timing his races, so I thought he might like it for when he gives the results next time."

"There's no answer to that," said Peter, breaking the silence which followed as everybody digested this latest piece of information.

"Do you mean to say," began one of the commissionaires, "that the whole of the Television Centre has been disrupted because of a bear's marmalade sandwich and a dud alarm clock?"

"Don't worry," said John, coming to Paddington's rescue. "I know one programme that's never been put off the air yet, and it won't be today — not if we hurry. Besides," he took the alarm clock from Paddington and examined it thoughtfully. "I've just had an idea. Has it ever struck anyone," he continued, "how many old alarm clocks there must be lying around in cupboards all over the country — just waiting to be disposed of?"

"There must be thousands," said Lesley.

"Full of brass cogs," added John.

"At least ten or a dozen in each," agreed Peter, as he began to realize what was in John's mind. "Not to mention all the other bits and pieces."

"There's gold in them thar works," said John. He turned back to Paddington. "We're always on the lookout for things to collect. It may not be much use for Desmond O'Donnelly any more, but it could be an idea for one of our future Appeals."

"And at least the BBC have tested the alarm

system," broke in Lesley. "We all know what to do now if there's ever a real bomb."

"That's all very well," broke in the taxi-driver as he pushed his way up to the front of the crowd. "But what about my fare? That's what I'd like to know. I reckon I could do with an appeal being launched for me. Paid me in matchsticks 'e did. *And* there's all me waiting time."

John felt in his pocket. "Have this one on Blue Peter," he said to Paddington. "One way and another I think we've all had our money's worth today, and after all, as the man said: 'None but the brave deserve the fare!' "

When John's remark had been explained to him even Paddington joined in the groans.

"I think," he announced, not to be outdone, "I'd like to clock in at the Television Centre every day of the week!"

CHAPTER FOUR

Paddington Passes Through

The commissionaire on duty outside the BBC Television Centre gazed doubtfully at the small figure standing in front of him.

"It's all highly irregular," he said. "By rights you should either have a pass issued by someone in authority, or ..." he made a stabbing motion with his forefinger in the direction of the main building, "*or*, I'm supposed to telephone the person or persons concerned in order to check your bona fides. For all I know," he added darkly, "they may not be quite what they're cracked up to be."

Paddington gave the man a hard stare. "My bona fides are cracked!" he exclaimed in alarm.

The commissionaire sighed. He was practically at the end of his period of duty and he had no wish to mar what had been an otherwise calm and trouble-free day by getting himself involved in a complicated discussion on the subject of bears' credentials.

"On the other hand," he continued hastily, "seeing as I know you by sight from your previous visits, and seeing as it's Friday and most of the office staff have gone home by now I reckon I could take a chance." He eyed Paddington through the gathering dusk. "I take it you do have some means of identification — just for the record?"

Paddington opened his suitcase and peered inside. "There's a photograph of my Aunt Lucy," he said. "No-one else has got one like that." He held it up for the man to see and then rummaged around still further. "Or there's this. It's got my paw mark on it."

The commissionaire gave a shudder as Paddington held up the squashed remains of a marmalade sandwich. "I don't suppose anyone else has got one like that either," he said with feeling.

Convinced beyond all shadow of doubt of his visitor's identity, the man disappeared inside his box and after consulting a list pinned to the wall came out again and handed Paddington a piece of paper with a figure written on it.

"That's the number of the studio you want," he said, as he raised the barrier. "You can leave your things there overnight, but mind you come straight out again ... and no touching anything."

Paddington returned the man's salute with a grateful raising of his hat. Then he picked up his suitcase with one paw and grasped the handle of his shopping basket on wheels with the other.

It took him a moment or two to get going as the basket was, to say the very least, somewhat over-laden. Over the years it had stood Paddington, not to mention the rest of the Brown family, in good stead fetching and carrying the weekly shopping between the Portobello Road and Windsor Gardens, but it was safe to say that during all that time it had probably never been quite so full.

It was piled high with an assortment of items ranging from mysterious packets tied up with string, through boxes of games and other pieces of bric-a-brac, to an old guitar which Jonathan had long since discarded and which was perched precariously on top.

It overflowed to such an extent Paddington found it difficult to see where he was going let alone where he had been, and on his way across the forecourt he had to stop several times in order to mop his brow. In doing so he somehow or other missed the main entrance to the Television Centre, and when he eventually stopped to check his whereabouts he found to his surprise that he had ended up outside some large doors at the back of the building.

Paddington was familiar with the layout of the BBC studios, and from past experience he remembered that these doors led straight into a wide circular corridor which ran round the outside of the building and was used to feed the different studios with scenery and other equipment.

As he came to a halt one of the doors slid back and a small electric trolley poked its nose out. It was towing a line of longer trucks laden with scenery, and as it slowed down to turn the corner the driver caught sight of Paddington and came to a halt alongside him.

"Can I help you, mate?" he called.

Paddington held his piece of paper up for the man to see. "I was looking for this studio," he announced.

The man gave it a brief glance and then took in Paddington's shopping basket on wheels. "Along there, second door on the left," he said, pointing along the corridor. "But you'd better hurry. The red light's flashing so they must be about to start. If I were you I'd leave your stuff just inside the door 'ere, grab your guitar and run."

"They're about to have a jam session," called another man, who was helping load some scenery on to a second truck.

"A jam session?" Paddington licked his lips as he propped his basket against the wall where the first man had suggested. "If I'd known I'd have brought a sliced loaf with me."

The driver scratched his head as Paddington hurried off up the corridor clutching his guitar. "Rum lot these folk singers," he said. "Talk a language all their own."

"A good shave wouldn't do some of 'em any harm," agreed the second man in a loud voice.

But if he was trying to make any sort of point he was wasting his time, for Paddington was already disappearing through the door leading to the studio. There was a momentary blast of music and then, as the door swung shut behind him, the red light which had been winking furiously before-hand glowed steadily to show that the programme was on the air.

Once inside, Paddington picked his way across a maze of cables and round several lots of scenery, until he finally found himself standing near a stage alongside two men, one of whom was wearing head-phones. A few feet away another man in evening dress was poised on a rostrum before a group of musicians.

As Paddington arrived the man brought the music to an end with a wave of his hand and then stepped down and beckoned towards the wings.

"Ladies and Gentlemen," he announced, as the cameras and microphone boom moved in, "this *is* Sonny Climes speaking. Now, I would like to pre-sent my first guest of the evening ..."

Feeling most surprised Paddington pushed his way past the two men and hurried across the studio floor.

He raised his hat several times in the direction of some applause which rose from the darkness beyond and then held out his paw.

"Good evening, Mr Climes," he said. "I've come about the jam."

Sonny Climes' jaw, which had dropped more than somewhat on catching sight of Paddington, now fell even further. "You've come about the jam?" he repeated. "*What* jam?"

In asking Paddington about the jam Sonny Climes made it sound as if it was only the first of many questions hovering on his lips, and that finding other things to ask was likely to be the least of his problems. But certainly, had he suffered any kind of shortage, he could have found eager and willing assistance from more than one person only a short bus ride away.

Back at number thirty-two Windsor Gardens the Browns gazed in horror at their television receiver.

"Crumbs!" exclaimed Jonathan. "Paddington!"

It was an obvious remark to make, but one which needed saying if only to confirm the fact that they were all seeing the same picture on their screen.

"I knew we shouldn't have let that bear go off to the Television Centre by himself," said Mrs Bird. "Something always happens when he's left to his own devices."

"Ssh!" said Mr Brown. "I think the conductor is saying something."

Trying to make the best of a bad job, Sonny Climes sought in the dark recesses of his mind for a tune which might have something to do with jam and which would suit his unexpected guest.

"Do you by any chance know '*It must be jelly 'cause jam don't shake like that*'?" he asked hopefully, at the same time giving a signal to the band.

There was a rustle of music as Paddington

considered the matter. "Perhaps it's the heat from the lights," he said. "Some of Mrs Bird's marmalade goes very wobbly in the hot weather — especially the sort without many chunks in it."

The rustling of paper in the background grew more frantic.

"I don't think that's in our repertoire," said Mr Climes in a voice which was growing more and more high pitched. "But we could have a go. Is it in A Flat?"

It was Paddington's turn to look puzzled. "No," he said firmly. "It's at number thirty-two Windsor Gardens."

Paddington was beginning to share Mr Climes' unhappiness about the way things were going. Out of the corner of his eye he could just see the man with the headphones. He was waving his arms about in a way which made Magnus Pyke look like a tailor's dummy, pointing first at the man standing beside him and then at the conductor.

"I think," announced Paddington, "I may go and get some sandwiches in the canteen instead, Mr Climes." And with that he turned on his heels and hurried off the set in the opposite direction to the way he'd come. He didn't like the expression on the studio manager's face at all, and he disappeared into the corridor as fast as his legs would carry him.

It was as he did so that he had his second shock of the evening; one moreover which caused him to stop dead in his tracks as if the whole world was about to collapse about his ears.

Only a few minutes before the corridor had been a hive of activity; now it was quiet and deserted, stripped bare of all the piles of scenery and props which had lined its walls. But it wasn't the absence of scenery or those who'd been moving it that caused Paddington's alarm, it was the fact that his shopping basket on wheels had disappeared as well.

For a moment or two he gazed at the spot where it had been as if he could hardly believe his eyes, then he pulled himself together and a purposeful look came over his face; one which boded ill for anyone who got between him and his objective.

Unaware of the drama that was taking place, the Browns continued their council of war back at number thirty-two Windsor Gardens.

"What *shall* we do?" asked Mrs Brown.

"I don't see what we *can* do," said Mr Brown. "What's he doing there anyway?"

"Goodness only knows," said Mrs Brown. "He spent the morning rummaging about in the attic and that's usually a bad sign."

"Knowing that bear," said Mrs Bird, "I'm sure he'll tell us all about it in his own good time, and I'm equally sure there are those at this very moment who are quite capable of putting things to rights."

Mrs Bird spoke with a confidence she didn't entirely feel, and if the caption on their screen saying that normal service would be resumed as soon as possible was anything to go by, the shock waves of Paddington's unexpected appearance were still reverberating around the Television Centre as well. Even the announcer seemed to have lost his usual calm and he apologized several times for putting on a record at the wrong speed.

"Perhaps we should try BBC2?" suggested Jonathan. "It's the story of Samuel Pepys."

"Anything's better than this," agreed Mr Brown, as he got up to press the button.

Trying hard to dismiss the matter from their minds the Browns settled back in their chairs in an attempt to adjust themselves mentally to the change of programme.

They appeared to have tuned in at a fairly quiet moment in the play, for Mr Pepys was standing at a high desk near the window of his lodgings, clasping a quill pen in his hand while he gazed reflectively through some French windows leading to the garden outside.

"Methinks," he began. "Methinks I see ..." Even as he began to speak Mr Pepys' eyes took on a slightly glazed look.

Unlike most programmes, which were pre-recorded, the Samuel Pepys serial was going out live. It was all part of a plan to borrow from some of the more popular children's programmes like Blue Peter and inject some excitement into the stories, but if the look on Mr Pepys' face at that moment was anything to go by he would have been much happier to settle for a quiet recorded life.

He mopped his brow with a kerchief and with a trembling hand dipped his quill into the ink again. "Methinks," he repeated, "I saw a bear go past the window. It was wearing a duffle-coat and an old hat and it was carrying some kind of suitcase. Perhaps," he said hopefully, turning to the camera, "it belonged to some strolling players and has gone on its way never to be seen again?"

But Mr Pepys hoped in vain. Before he had a chance to recharge his quill, let alone pen any more thoughts in his diary, there was a knock at the door, followed by a flurry of movement from the cameras as they changed position to take in this unexpected development.

"Good evening," said Paddington, raising his hat as he entered the room.

"Er ... good morrow," said the luckless author desperately. He gave a deep bow. "Samuel Pepys ..."

"Does he really?" said Paddington. He gave the

man a hard stare. "Mrs Bird says that's rude."

"Er ... Mistress Bird?" said the actor desperately. "Verily I do not think I know the wench."

"*Wench!*" repeated Paddington hotly. "Mrs Bird isn't a wench!"

"Perhaps," said the man hastily as Paddington gave him another hard stare, "perhaps I could read to you from my diary?"

Paddington considered the matter for a moment. "It's very kind of you," he said at last. "If I had the time I could read to you from my scrapbook as well. Only I'm in a hurry. I'm afraid I've lost something very important."

"Oh dear. Can I help you?" said Mr Pepys, clutching at straws.

"I don't think so," replied Paddington gloomily. He cast his eyes round Mr Pepys' room. "I don't think what I want has been invented yet!"

The babble of noise which emerged from the dozens of pairs of headphones being worn by the technicians in the studio was equalled only by the groan which rose from the living room of number thirty-two Windsor Gardens as they took in this latest piece of news.

"We *must* do something," said Mrs Brown. "We can't just leave him there to his own devices. There's no knowing what he'll do next."

Mrs Bird rose to her feet. "I'm going to make

some 'phone calls," she said. "There's not much point in having friends in high places if you can't call on them in times of emergency."

Mrs Bird hurried from the room. Through Paddington's many escapades in the past she had acquired quite a few telephone numbers, mostly those of the members of the Blue Peter team, and she felt sure that they would be only too pleased to help in any way possible.

But on her return to the living room Mrs Bird's face looked, if anything, even longer than it had when she left.

"Not a single reply," she said. "They must all be out."

"Well," said Mrs Brown, trying to strike a cheerful note. "No news is good news."

"Talking of which," said Mr Brown, as he pressed a button on the television and some music burst forth, "perhaps we could try watching the nine o'clock news. They may mention something on that."

The music faded as a picture of Angela Rippon filled the screen, and with her customary air of calm managed to convey the feeling that even if all was not entirely well with the world at large at least things were reasonably safe for the time being. Once again the Browns settled back and found themselves lulled into a sense of security as the day's events unfolded before their eyes.

It was as she neared the end of the programme and began reciting the main points of the news again that Miss Rippon's eyes took on a slightly glazed look. She shifted uneasily in her chair as a shadow fell across the scenery behind her, hovered for a moment, disappeared, then appeared again.

"And that," she said quickly but firmly, "is the end of the news."

At the sound of her words the shadow sprang to life with a clearly visible raising of a hat. "No it isn't," called a voice.

"Crikey!" groaned Jonathan. "Here he comes again!"

"Excuse me, Miss Rippon!" cried Paddington hotly as he came into view, "before you finish the news I've got another main point. Someone's taken my shopping basket on wheels!"

Paddington looked as if he was about to address the nation at great length on the subject, but by now the engineers were more than ready for any emergency, and before he had a chance to say any more the picture faded from the screen.

"So that's it!" exclaimed Judy. "No wonder he's upset."

"Only Paddington could lose a shopping basket on wheels in the Television Centre," said Jonathan. "I wouldn't mind betting he'll put in a lot more appearances before the end of the evening," he added, trying to keep the note of hope from his voice.

Mrs Bird rose to her feet. "Not if I have anything to do with it," she said grimly. "I don't know what the rest of you are doing, but *I'm* off to the BBC."

The Director for the Evaluation of Audience Figures bounded out from behind his desk as Paddington entered the room, closely followed by a throng of other people.

"Good evening," he said, holding out his hand. "I'm D.E.A.F."

"Oh dear!" said Paddington. "I'm sorry about that." He rummaged for a moment or two in his newly recovered shopping basket on wheels and then withdrew a large metal funnel. "Perhaps you'd like to use this," he shouted at the top of his voice, as he placed the small end to his lips and directed the large end towards the man's head. "It's an old one of Mrs Bird's, but it makes a very good ear trumpet."

John, Peter and Lesley exchanged glances with the Browns as the Director staggered back clutching his ear. They could sense the start of some complicated misunderstandings, and there had been enough of those already that evening. Enough, that is, to send all those present rushing post haste to the Television Centre in the hope of averting any more disasters.

John cupped a hand to his mouth. "He's not deaf," he hissed. "He's D.E.A.F. — that's not the same thing at all. People are always using initials at the BBC." He was about to add that they usually did so because it saved time, but catching sight of the expression on Paddington's face he decided that it might not always hold true.

"Perhaps you would like to tell us your story in your own words?" said the Director, addressing Paddington, as he retired to the safety of his desk.

Paddington considered the matter for a moment. So much had happened that evening he wasn't quite sure where to begin. "Well," he said, "I'm P.B. and I come from D.P. I brought my S.B.O.W. to the BBC because I wanted to be ready for the M.C.S.S. tomorrow."

If Paddington thought his explanation would

help clear the air he was doomed to disappointment.

"Er ... would you mind repeating that in plain language?" asked the Director of Audience Figures.

Paddington gave the man a funny look. For someone who liked using initials he didn't seem to know much about them.

"I'm Paddington Brown," he explained patiently, "and I come from Darkest Peru. I brought my shopping basket on wheels to the BBC and I left it in a corridor with some scenery while I went into a studio by mistake, and when I came out again it had gone, so I've been looking for it ever since."

Peter glanced at Paddington's basket. "If you left that out in the scenery corridor," he said, "no wonder it disappeared. They probably thought it was being used in Going for a Song."

"Going for a Song?" repeated Paddington hotly. "I was hoping to get more for it than that. It was meant for the M.C.S.S."

"The M.C.S.S.?" chorused everyone else in the room.

"What's that when it's at home?" exclaimed Mr Brown.

Paddington gave a deep sigh. He was beginning to wish people would make up their minds exactly what they *did* want from him. One moment it was initials, the next moment it wasn't.

"The M.C.S.S. is the Multi-Coloured Swap Shop," he explained patiently. "I had rather a lot of things to swap so I thought I would bring them along the night before just to make sure. The man at the gate gave me a piece of paper with the number of the studio on. It was Studio 6 only I must have held it upside down because I went in Number 9 by mistake."

The silence which greeted Paddington's latest announcement was broken by Mrs Brown. "I'm very sorry about all this," she exclaimed, turning to the Director. "We had no idea ..."

"Sorry?" repeated the Director of Audience Figures. "My dear lady, there's no need to be sorry." He jumped to his feet again. "Why, it's the best thing that's happened to me in years. The reason I asked you all up here is so that I can congratulate this young bear personally. Since he arrived at the studios we've been flooded with reports from all over the country about people tuning in to see when and where he's going to appear next. Word gets around you know. Why, the news got a bigger audience than the World Cup, and we've had a lot of complaints because we faded it."

He turned back to Paddington and looked at him wistfully. "I wish we could find a way of fitting you into our schedules every night of the year," he exclaimed. "It would probably mean promotion."

"I could start now if you like," said Paddington eagerly. "It's quite easy really. All you do is go in through doors. If I hurry I might be in time for Sky at Night."

"Er, yes," said the Director hastily. "On the other hand there's a lot to be said for keeping people guessing and enough's as good as a feast. Talking of which, I wonder if you would all care to join me in a little something before we turn in? I daresay you could do with some refreshment."

"A marmalade sandwich?" suggested John, giving the others a wink.

"Followed by a nice cup of hot cocoa?" added Lesley.

"You'll need building up if you're going to be on the M.C.S.S. tomorrow morning," agreed Peter. "It starts early."

Paddington considered the matter for a moment. What with one thing and another, it *had* been a busy time and he was feeling very hungry.

"I think," he announced to everyone's relief, "that's a very good idea. There's nothing like rounding things off with a M.S. and a C.O.H.C. before you go to B. Especially," he added, gazing round at all his friends, "when you can share it with Fs like J.P. and Miss J. from B.P., not to mention all the Bs from W.G.!"

CHAPTER FIVE

Paddington Takes a Cut

As the familiar strains of the Blue Peter — Special Assignment signature tune came to an end, Paddington switched off the Browns' television receiver and then sat back in his armchair with a thoughtful expression on his face.

Paddington liked the Blue Peter — Special Assignment films. Over the years Valerie Singleton had visited most of the capitals of Europe and he now felt as though *he* knew them all even better through seeing them on television than he would have done had he been lucky enough to visit them himself.

The nice thing about the films was that they were

so packed with information no matter how many times you saw them there was always something new to be learnt.

On this particular occasion there had been an item about topiary — the art of clipping shrubs and hedges into fantastic shapes — and although he knew he must have seen it before, somehow or other it suddenly seemed completely fresh.

During Valerie's visit to some gardens on the continent she had come across a whole area — a kind of 'secret garden' — devoted to hedges and shrubs which over the years had been trimmed into all sorts of shapes; geometrical patterns, tables and chairs, not to mention birds and animals of various kinds. There had even been a bear; and towards the end of the film, through the use of trick photography, Valerie had pretended to have an encounter with an elephant. It wasn't until she'd tried to feed it with a bun that some leaves had fallen off its trunk and the secret had been revealed.

In the normal course of events Paddington wasn't the keenest of gardeners, which was probably why the item hadn't caught his attention the first time round. He liked playing with the hosepipe and picking raspberries during the season, but when it came to carrying out day-to-day tasks, like mowing the lawn and keeping the hedges trimmed, he usually managed to find other more important things to do. However, the idea of actually clipping a bush to make it appear like something else struck him as a very interesting one indeed.

After considering the matter for a moment or two Paddington stood up again. Although Valerie hadn't had time to go into all the details of topiary, he felt sure his friend, Mr Gruber, would be able to help.

A few minutes later there was a click from the front door of number thirty-two Windsor Gardens as it closed behind him and he set off in the direction of the market.

Mr Gruber's antique shop in the Portobello Road was a veritable treasure trove of good things, and apart from all the old furniture, and the copper, silver, brass and china objects which filled it almost to overflowing, the walls themselves were lined with shelves containing books on practically every subject under the sun.

Over the years Paddington had consulted Mr Gruber on a good many occasions and sure enough, no sooner had he voiced his latest request, than his friend reached up to a shelf somewhere near the back of the shop and took down a slim volume with a picture of a rather leafy-looking peacock on the jacket.

"I think you'll find all you want to know in here, Mr Brown," he said. "It's called *Clippings from*

My Hedgerow and it's by Ebenezer Hawthorne."

Mr Gruber went on to explain that Mr Hawthorne was very well known in gardening circles for his work with shrubs and that his designs were to be found in some of the best gardens in England.

"But be careful, Mr Brown," he warned, as Paddington made ready to leave. "Don't forget — what comes off won't always go back on again."

Paddington thanked his friend for his help and advice, and after raising his hat he turned and hurried back in the direction of Windsor Gardens again. He was the sort of bear who believed in striking while the iron was hot and with the sun already well past its peak there was no time to be lost.

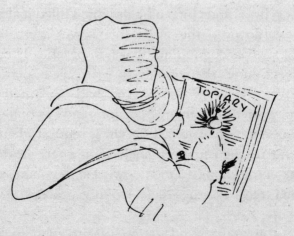

To his relief the Browns were nowhere to be seen when he arrived home. Although, by and large, he was allowed a fairly free paw in the garden, from past experience he felt it might be better if he presented them with a finished work rather than try to explain what his intentions were.

He spent some while in the shed poring over his new book, and when he finally emerged carrying Mr Brown's best shears in one paw and a large sheet of paper in the other, there was a determined gleam in his eye.

Mr Hawthorne was nothing if not thorough in his description of how to go about matters, and in the end Paddington had confined himself to making copies of some of the many illustrations which graced the pages of the book. In particular there was a photograph of a large bear which the author had fashioned for his own garden and which was apparently so life-like even his own dog gave it a wide berth.

After making a few passing snips through the air in order to get used to handling the shears, Paddington looked around in search of a suitable subject for his attentions. Most of Mr Brown's shrubs were either of the flowering variety and rather spindly, or they were so short they wouldn't have lent themselves to being shaped into a hedgehog, let alone anything on two legs.

Apart from that, according to Ebenezer Hawthorne, far and away the best place for a work of topiary was in the centre of a lawn where it could be seen from all angles, and in the end, much to his disappointment, Paddington had to settle for an old yew bush which was growing alongside the garden fence.

Taking a deep breath, he stood on tiptoe and snipped at one of the topmost twigs.

Almost immediately he regretted his action, for there came a bellow of rage from the other side of the fence and to his horror the Browns' neighbour, Mr Curry, rose into view clutching his eye.

"Bear!" roared Mr Curry, as he focused his gaze on Paddington. "What are you doing now, bear? Something hit me in the eye just then!"

"It's topiary, Mr Curry," cried Paddington, trying to hide the shears under his duffle-coat. "It was only a twig and I didn't mean it to go over your fence. I didn't know you were spying ... I mean ..." He broke off as Mr Curry's face started to change colour.

"*Toe* parings!" bellowed the Browns' neighbour. "How dare you throw toe parings over my fence!"

"Not toe parings, Mr Curry," exclaimed Paddington. "To*piary*. That's quite a different thing. It's to do with cutting shrubs. I'm making a bear ... look!" And he held his sheet of paper up in the air to show what he meant.

"A bear?" snorted Mr Curry, as he peered at Paddington's drawing. "I don't see what you want to make a *bear* for. The place is enough of a bear garden already without making it worse."

"Oh, I can do lots of other things, Mr Curry," said Paddington confidently. "Peacocks, elephants, kangaroos ..." His face fell. "The only trouble is I haven't got any proper bushes to work on."

Mr Curry grabbed the piece of paper and stared at it. "I didn't know you went in for this sort of thing, bear," he growled.

"Bears are good at cutting things, Mr Curry," said Paddington, waving his shears in the air again.

"Hmm. Yes. ... well ... watch what you're doing." Mr Curry stepped back a pace and eyed

Paddington thoughtfully. "I wouldn't mind a bit of topiary in *my* garden," he continued. "A peacock in the middle of the lawn might raise the tone a bit, and it just so happens that I have a bush that needs pruning.

"Mind you," the Browns' neighbour looked round to make sure no-one else was listening and then beckoned Paddington to come closer, "I wouldn't want every Tom, Dick and Harry to have one. I'd like mine to be exclusive. If I had one that was exclusive it's quite possible I might not mention your trying to poke my eye out with a stick just now."

"Oh, I'm sure yours would be exclusive, Mr Curry," said Paddington, anxious to make amends. "I'd make sure yours would be like nothing else that had ever been done before."

"Hmm." Mr Curry came to a decision. "In that case, bear," he said, lifting some boards in the fence to one side, "you can start right away. I shall leave you to it while I go out and get some ointment for my eye before the shops close."

Paddington needed no second bidding and a few moments later, almost before the sound of Mr Curry's side gate being slammed shut had died away, he was hard at work.

At first sight, Mr Curry's bush had all the signs of being a very promising model to work on indeed.

82

Apart from the fact that it was ideally situated in the middle of the lawn, it had been untouched for so long it was positively crying out for someone to give it a trim.

Paddington consulted his drawing several times to get the feel of things and then made the first few cuts. It was really very satisfying and he could quite see why Mr Hawthorne had found so much to write about on the subject. In one chapter of his book called *Nature's Hairdresser*, he had likened the whole business to that of cutting hair. First there was the general styling, then there was a long period of touching-up, endlessly snipping bits off here and there in order to reach a state of perfection.

In the case of Mr Curry's bush the general styling was over in no time at all. In fact, had he been there to see it even the Browns' neighbour would have been hard put to find fault. Really and truly, although it might not have taken in another peacock who happened to be passing, the end result did bear a striking resemblance to the one shown on the front of Mr Gruber's book.

It was when Paddington turned his attention to the final touching up process that he began to experience trouble. Another of Mr Hawthorne's hobby horses was the care one had to take in order to avoid upsetting the balance of nature. In Paddington's case it wasn't so much nature itself he was worried about, it was the balance of Mr Curry's peacock. No sooner had he snipped a piece off one side than he found he had to snip a piece off the other.

Gradually the pile of clippings by his side grew larger and larger, but it wasn't until he stood up and moved back a few paces to view the end result that he realized with a start just how much he *had* taken off.

Paddington gazed mournfully at what was left of Mr Curry's bush. Any resemblance it once might have had to a bird had long since gone. Even allowing for the failing light, it was definitely more pea than cock. In fact, not to put too fine a point on it, there was little more than a stump left in the ground, and even Mr Hawthorne himself would have been hard put to fashion more than a bedraggled sparrow out of the remains, let alone anything larger.

Paddington sat down and peered hopefully at his book, but as if to rub salt into his wound almost the first words he read were the ominous ones: "Some of the simpler shapes can be completed in as short a time as ten years."

"Ten *years*!" exclaimed Paddington, addressing the world in general as the book fell from his paws.

From the expression on his face in the accompanying illustration, Mr Hawthorne obviously thought that even that length of time was pretty good going, but equally obvious was the fact that he'd been living in balmier days, untroubled by next door neighbours like Mr Curry. As far as Paddington was concerned any solution to his problem which took more than ten minutes was cause for alarm, and as even that amount of time began to dwindle away his face grew longer and longer.

Although he'd promised the Browns' neighbour that his bush would end up looking like no-one else's, Paddington had a nasty feeling Mr Curry would be far from happy with the result, and by now there were so many twigs and branches lying on the ground the chances of glueing them back together in anything like the right order seemed very remote indeed.

In the past Paddington had often found that when things were at their very worst something often happened to make them come right again; almost as if, like Mr Hawthorne's belief in the balance of nature, some unseen force came to the rescue in order to tip the scales in the opposite direction, and it was as he gazed around Mr Curry's garden that a gleam of hope suddenly came into his eyes.

The Browns' neighbour had obviously recently taken delivery of something big, for beside the dustbin there was a large pile of white packing material. The sight of it reminded Paddington of an item he'd seen a few weeks before on Blue Peter; an item which at the time he'd found very interesting, but for one reason or another had never followed up.

He scrambled to his feet. Desperate situations demanded desperate measures, and with Mr Curry already overdue from his visit to the chemist there wasn't a moment to lose. Soon, the only sound which broke the silence was that of heavy breathing, intermingled with a strange squeaking sound as Paddington set to work again.

Mr Curry gazed approvingly at the result of Paddington's labours. "I must say I take my hat off to you, bear," he said grudgingly. "That peacock is one of the best I've ever seen outside of a zoo.

"In fact," he continued, with a sudden burst of generosity, "if you come and see me tomorrow I might even give you fivepence for your trouble."

"Thank you very much, Mr Curry," said Paddington gratefully. "Perhaps you'd like to give it to me now?" he added hopefully. "You might not want to in the morning."

The Browns' neighbour glared at Paddington through the gathering dusk. "Nonsense, bear!" he growled, banging his hand on the top of the bush in order to emphasize his words. "Why shouldn't I want to? If I say I'm going to do a thing I do it. Are you suggesting I'm the sort of person who goes back on his word? Why, I'll have you know . . ."

Whatever else Mr Curry had been about to say was lost for all time as he brought his hand down again and suddenly encountered empty air.

Turning round, he gazed disbelievingly at the

spot where a moment before the peacock had stood, and then at the sight of it bouncing across the lawn, shedding leaves and branches as it gathered speed and headed towards the fence.

"Bear!" he bellowed, when he found his voice at last. "Come back, bear!"

But he was too late. Paddington was already fleeing from the scene. There was a momentary pause by the fence as he scrambled to get both himself and the bird through the gap at the same time, and then he disappeared from view.

Fivepence or no fivepence, quite clearly Mr Hawthorne had lost one of his readers for the rest of that day, if not for all time.

"Lots of you will probably remember," said Lesley, as she turned to face the camera, "that a few weeks ago we did an item on carving polystyrene — the material which turns up as packing in practically everything you buy these days and which always seems to end up being thrown out for the dustmen.

"A lot of you sent in pictures of the things you made after the programme ... cars, trains ... there was even a model of the Television Centre here in Wood Lane, but today we've got something really special to show you."

As the camera zoomed out to a wider shot, Lesley stood up and strolled across to a rostrum where a large and impressive looking green object was on display.

"It's a peacock ... carved entirely by paw and decorated with real leaves. I'm afraid some of them have dried out under the heat of the studio lights, but it's so unusual we felt sure you'd like to meet the owner, so we've asked him along to the studio today ..."

"Good Heavens!"

"Paddington!"

A cry of amazement went up from the Brown household as the Director cut away to another picture and the familiar figure of Paddington appeared on their screen.

"No wonder that bear wanted us to watch Blue Peter," said Mrs Bird. "I had a feeling he had something up his sleeve."

"And what's he doing with a peacock?" said Jonathan. "I didn't know he even liked birds."

"Ssh!" broke in Judy. "Lesley's telling us."

The Browns fell silent as Lesley guided Paddington through the various stages of his model; how he had carved the peacock out of several pieces of polystyrene tied together, and how he'd then covered it by pushing leaves and twigs from Mr Curry's bush into the material.

89

"I must say it was very kind of Mr Curry to let you do all that," said Lesley.

"Well, he didn't actually *let* me, Miss Judd," admitted Paddington. "It was a bit of a surprise. It sort of happened."

"Oh Lord," groaned Mr Brown. "Here we go again."

"Quiet, Henry," broke in Mrs Brown. "We don't want to miss anything."

"Talking of things which have happened," said Lesley, turning to the camera, "we have a surprise here in the studio now. We all thought Paddington's model was such a good idea we decided to make one for ourselves. In fact, we've gone one better — with the aid of a few bits and pieces from the Blue Peter garden we've made one that's actually alive."

"Mercy me!" Mrs Bird nearly dropped her knitting as the picture on their screen changed yet again. "If that's not Paddington it's his double."

The Browns sat glued to their seats as the camera, which had started by showing a wide shot of the studio, moved steadily in towards a gaily coloured object standing apart from all the rest. From a distance it had indeed looked remarkably like Paddington, but as it began to fill the screen they could see that it was almost entirely covered with flowers.

"You see," said Lesley, as she talked over the

picture for the benefit of viewers at home, "what we've done is take Paddington's idea a stage further. We've made large holes all over the model we built of him and we've filled them with pots of flowers ... blue ones for the duffle-coat ... dark, almost black pansies for the hat ... and brown foliage for the fur. We've even ..." Lesley paused in order to allow the Director to cut to a close-up of an orange-coloured jar, "we've even used marigolds for the marmalade pot.

"Now," she asked, as the rest of the team joined her in sitting alongside Paddington ready to close the show, "what do you think of that?

"Or, perhaps more to the point," she added, "what are you going to do with it?"

Oblivious of the studio manager making frantic wind-up signs alongside the camera taking his picture, Paddington considered the matter very carefully before replying. When he'd taken his model of the peacock along to the Blue Peter offices he'd had no idea quite so many things would happen and he wanted to make sure he did the right thing.

"I think," he announced at last, much to everyone's relief, "I shall give it to Mr and Mrs Brown's next door neighbour. I promised him he would have something unique, and I don't think even Mr Curry could grumble when he sees what I've brought him."

CHAPTER SIX

Paddington's Christmas Treasure Hunt

Mrs Brown opened the kitchen window of number thirty-two Windsor Gardens and gazed out with a puzzled expression on her face.

"That's very strange," she said. "Fancy hearing a bumblebee at this time of year. It's only two weeks to Christmas."

Mrs Bird joined her at the sink and cupped one hand to her ear. Sure enough, the quiet of the afternoon was suddenly broken into by a loud buzzing noise. If it was a bumblebee it was certainly one which was suffering from the effects of the weather, for every so often the buzz developed into a spluttering wheeze, followed by an ominous silence as if it was gathering its second wind before continuing a fruitless search for the last rose of summer.

For a moment or two the Browns' housekeeper looked as puzzled as Mrs Brown. Then, as her sharp eyes caught a movement behind some shrubs, followed by a momentary glimpse of a familiar-looking blue duffle-coat, her face cleared.

"That's not a bumblebee," she said, as she returned to her baking. "That's Paddington. He must be having another look for buried treasure with Mr Brown's Magic-probe."

"Is that all?" Mrs Brown looked relieved as she closed the window. Mrs Bird's remark had solved two problems which had been bothering her. One was the noise of the "bee"; the other was the lack of noise from Paddington. Mrs Brown always felt uneasy when Paddington was quiet for too long a time. It usually meant he was "up to something".

"All the same," she glanced out of the window again, "I do hope he's wrapped up well. We don't want him in bed with a cold over Christmas."

"Hmm!" Mrs Bird gave a snort. "I doubt if he'll be out there very long. Too many people have been over the ground before. I'll match Paddington's weight in marmalade against any treasure he finds buried."

Having made her pronouncement Mrs Bird went back to work with the air of one confident that her predictions would come true. In saying that the garden at number thirty-two Windsor Gardens had been "gone over", the Browns' housekeeper was speaking from practical experience, for she had been one of the first to join in the general excitement when Mr Brown received a metal detector for his birthday.

In the event the "Magic-probe" had proved something of a nine-days' wonder. Apart from a few old tools which had lain buried over the years, the garden had yielded up very little in the way of objects of value, and after Paddington had dug up a telephone cable by mistake one morning, the detector had been put into cold storage by general consent to await better weather and the prospect of trips to the seaside.

"Not," said Mrs Bird, "that I wouldn't put it past that bear to come up with something. He has the luck of Old Nick."

Unaware that he was the object of some discussion in the kitchen, Paddington settled himself down behind the raspberry canes and gazed disconsolately at a small booklet he held in his paw.

It was called *Every Man a Treasure Island* and it was written by a Mr Arnold Prosper. The picture on the front cover showed Mr Prosper dressed in

Elizabethan costume clutching one of his probes like a buccaneer fresh from doing battle with the Spanish Fleet and surrounded by the spoils of battle.

According to the foreword, most people, if they did but know it, were standing on something of value. Doubloons, sovereigns, items of bronze, silver and other precious metals; Mr Prosper had amassed so much during his career he had a job to squeeze them all into the many photographs in his book. Looking at his own "spoils" — several rusty nails, an old bicycle pedal and a horseshoe — Paddington had to admit he would have been hard put to fill a postage stamp let alone anything larger.

Heaving a deep sigh he opened his suitcase and turned his attention to a glossy pamphlet which he withdrew from the secret compartment. Paddington was very keen on brochures and he often sent away for them. They were a good way of finding out about things and over the years he'd formed a large collection. But this particular one was unsolicited and had arrived through the post several days before. Most of one side was taken up by a picture of a cake; but not just any old cake — a very unusual kind called *Auntie Mabel's Pecan Nut Special*.

According to the wording on the back, Auntie Mabel and her team of willing helpers had been hard at work for some months baking them ready for the coming holiday season. And if the number of glowing testimonials from satisfied customers who'd ordered them the year before was anything to go by, no Christmas could possibly be complete without one.

With Christmas not far away Paddington was already well into his shopping, but not for the first time he was at a loss to know what to buy the Blue Peter team. Blue Peter had always been rather a problem. Over the years his circle of friends on the programme had grown and grown, and although he was a generous bear at heart it had become impossible to buy each and every one of them a present.

A cake had seemed like a very good idea indeed. Looking at the picture again Paddington felt sure that with careful slicing they could all have one, if not two, pieces for their Christmas tea.

Unfortunately, like all good things in life there was a price to pay, and although Auntie Mabel was at pains to point out that with the cost of pecan nuts going up all the time, ten pounds — including postage and packing — was a mere trifle, it was far beyond Paddington's means. His Christmas savings had already been severely dented following a bout of present buying for the Brown family, and they were in very definite need of an injection of ready cash.

The need for prompt action had caused him to pay a visit to his friend Mr Gruber, who kept an antique shop in the Portobello Road. Mr Gruber was always willing and able to give advice on practically every subject under the sun, and once again he'd turned up trumps. From among the many books lining his shelves he'd produced an A–Z on unusual careers.

Unfortunately, however, like many of his books, its value lay in its age and most of the jobs covered belonged to more leisured times. Having rejected in quick succession possible careers in Bath Management, Deep Sea Diving and Lighthouse Keeping — all of which seemed to need long periods of training — Paddington had been about to give up when he'd caught sight of a section on Gold Prospecting, and this in turn had reminded him of Mr Brown's Magic-probe.

Returning to his instruction book, Paddington leafed through a section at the end where, in a series of pictures, Mr Prosper made the point that some of his best finds had come about largely by accident. One photograph even showed him tossing a coin over his shoulder in order to mark the spot for his next "dig". Three pictures later, dressed this time as Long John Silver with a parrot on his shoulder, he was shown holding up a large silver plate worth, so the caption said, several hundred pounds.

Closing his eyes, Paddington lay back amongst the raspberries and tried to picture the scene. Despite the time of year, the search for buried treasure had made him feel quite hot. So much so he loosened one of the toggles on his duffle-coat as he rested his head against one of the canes. As his paw dropped limply to the ground he felt it come up against something cold and hard, and gradually an idea floated into his mind.

If Arnold Prosper had achieved so much success simply by throwing a coin over his shoulder, who could tell what would happen with something really big; something as large as a horseshoe for example. It was the kind of thought which was difficult to resist, especially with matters reaching such a desperate stage.

Paddington was a hopeful bear at heart, but even he hadn't bargained on quite such a speedy result from his action — or such a noisy one.

The horseshoe hardly seemed to have left his paw when the air was torn asunder by a loud yell from somewhere close at hand.

"Bear!" came the familiar voice of the Browns' next door neighbour, Mr Curry. "Did you do that, bear?"

At first glance Mr Curry looked as if he had become inextricably attached to a pneumatic drill that had run amok, for he was bobbing up and

down on the other side of the fence like someone on a pogo stick. But closer inspection through a knot hole revealed that in fact he was hopping around his garden on one leg, clutching his other foot with both hands, his face getting redder and redder with every passing moment.

"Did you do that, bear?" he repeated, pointing a trembling finger at the offending horseshoe. "Because, if so ..."

"Oh, no, Mr Curry," explained Paddington, anxious to make amends. "I didn't actually *do* it. It just happened. Besides," he added brightly, as a sudden thought struck him. "Mrs Bird always says horseshoes are supposed to be lucky."

"Lucky!" bellowed Mr Curry. "*Lucky?*" He paused in his antics. "I don't call having a great lump of iron land on my foot lucky. I've a very good mind to . . ."

The Browns' neighbour broke off as he looked over the fence and caught sight of the various items of equipment lying on the ground where Paddington had left them.

"What have you got there, bear?" he demanded suspiciously.

"That's Mr Brown's Magic-probe, Mr Curry," said Paddington, only too pleased to change the subject. "I'm looking for treasure."

"Treasure?" Mr Curry hobbled closer to the fence in order to take a closer look. "What sort of treasure?"

"Oh, all sorts," exclaimed Paddington, warming to his subject. "Buried especially." He picked up the instruction book, which as luck would have it was still open at the page where Mr Prosper had found his silver plate. "That's why I threw the horseshoe — I wanted to see where to start my next sweep."

"Hmm." Mr Curry considered the matter for a moment or two, then he marched to the centre of the lawn and indicated the bedraggled remains of a flower bed which he'd just started to dig.

"Well, I suggest you start right now. If you manage to find anything — which I very much doubt, I *may* not report you for your dangerous behaviour just now."

Paddington needed no second bidding. Without so much as a backward glance towards the house he picked up his belongings and before the Browns' neighbour had a chance to change his mind, pushed aside some loose boards in the fence.

Although it was true to say that Mrs Bird thought highly of the lucky properties of horseshoes, she held equally strong views on the subject of those who threw things without looking first, and he had no wish to be reported — especially with Christmas so near at hand.

"Right." Mr Curry pointed to a dent in the ground where he was standing. "That's where it landed."

Paddington eyed the spot doubtfully as he began setting up his equipment. He'd seldom seen a less inviting patch of ground. Apart from a few earthworms who seemed relieved to be able to make good their escape now the soil had been turned over, it looked so barren even Mr Prosper might have been tempted to have another go with his coin.

"Perhaps you'd like to go indoors and wait while I make my search, Mr Curry?" he suggested hopefully.

The Browns' neighbour glared at him. "I shall do no such thing, bear!" he barked. "There's no knowing what sort of tricks you'd get up to once my back was turned."

"*Tricks*, Mr Curry?" Paddington looked most offended as he pressed the switch on Mr Brown's Magic-probe.

"Yes, bear, *tricks*." The Browns' neighbour looked as if he was about to compile a long list of things which might happen if Paddington was left to his own devices, but before he had a chance to make a start his words were drowned by a loud rasping noise from the probe.

"Good Heavens!" he exclaimed. "What was that?"

Paddington looked equally astonished. "I don't know, Mr Curry," he said excitedly. "I think it must be something very valuable indeed."

In his book of instructions Arnold Prosper had listed the various sounds the probe made whenever it came within range of any buried metal, so that a skilled operator could soon learn to tell the difference between worthless junk and items of value. But nowhere had he seen any mention of quite such a loud noise. Mr Prosper's noises ranged between the soft murmur of a gnat on a summer's day and a comb and paper, whereas the present one sounded more like a motor cycle that had gone wildly out of control during a TT race.

Switching it on again, he moved towards the spot where Mr Curry was standing. Immediately the rasping grew louder, until by the time he was directly over Mr Curry's feet it threatened to blow the very cone out of the loudspeaker, and he had to quickly turn the volume down.

Mr Curry's eyes nearly popped out of his head. "I take back all I said, bear," he remarked grudgingly. Then he looked round carefully to make sure no-one else could overhear. "We must keep this a secret — just between the two of us. We'll go shares on anything we find."

Paddington's face fell. Mr Curry's meanness was legendary in the neighbourhood, outweighed only by his bad temper, and from past experience he knew that any sharing would be very one-sided indeed.

But in the event whatever decision he might have come to would have mattered little, for the Browns' neighbour was already hard at work with his spade.

"Keep your eyes peeled, bear," he growled. "We don't want any interruptions. If you see anyone watching tell them to mind their own business."

"Yes, Mr Curry." Glad to be left to his own devices for a while, Paddington stood back and watched as the pile of earth grew larger and larger. Every so often, at Mr Curry's request, he switched on the probe and waved it to and fro across the spot where he was digging, and each time there was an answering buzz. If it didn't get any louder — which was scarcely possible — it certainly didn't get any less.

"Are you sure that thing's working properly?" gasped Mr Curry some while later, as he climbed out of the hole and stood mopping his brow like some early gold prospector in the grip of the fever.

"Oh, yes, Mr Curry," said Paddington. And to prove the matter beyond all doubt he demonstrated over the horseshoe which had started it all, and which now lay forgotten on the nearby lawn.

"Hmmm." The Browns' neighbour looked round at the gathering dusk and then came to a decision. "I'm going indoors to fetch a torch, bear," he announced. "I'm not giving up now. While I'm gone you can carry on with the digging. But as soon as you find anything," he warned, "stop immediately. I don't want you putting your spade through anything valuable."

As Mr Curry disappeared up the garden path Paddington lowered himself gently into the hole. It was a large hole — almost up to his shoulders, and he could quite see why Mr Curry looked so worn out. Reaching up for the Magic-probe, he decided to have one last quick check before he started work, but as he switched it on a worried expression came over his face.

Gone was the loud rasping noise of a few moments before. In its place was the familiar low-pitched burr which showed that the machine was working, but nothing more.

He tried switching it on and off several times, but all to no avail, and even turning the volume up and shaking it produced nothing more than a few crackles.

Paddington gazed in growing alarm, first at the end of the probe, and then at the bottom of the hole. Mr Curry's treasure seemed to have vanished into thin air. Worse still, before he had time to investigate the matter there came a tramping of feet and the Browns' neighbour arrived back on the scene.

"Bear!" he barked. "Why aren't you digging, bear?"

"I was just about to, Mr Curry," cried Paddington, blinking in the light from the torch. "Except there's no need now. At least . . ." He broke off as simultaneously with the Magic-probe bursting into life again he caught sight of something — a momentary gleam — which made his stomach turn to water.

"No need to?" bellowed Mr Curry. "What do you mean — there's no need to?"

He stared down at Paddington. "What's up, bear? Is anything the matter? And what are you doing — waving that thing about in the air? The treasure's under *your* feet — not mine."

"I don't think so, Mr Curry," said Paddington mournfully, as the awful truth dawned on him. "I think we've been getting signals from your studs."

"My *studs*?" repeated Mr Curry. "What studs?"

"The studs on your boots," said Paddington. "That's why it always sounded as if the treasure was under your feet no matter how deep down you went. Mr Prosper says you have to watch out for these things. If you look in the instruction book you'll . . ." He broke off from his explanations as a gasp of strangled rage came from somewhere overhead. Even without the aid of the torch the look on Mr Curry's face would have been frightening to behold; caught in the rays as he waved it to and fro it was positively menacing.

"Bear!" he bellowed. "Bear . . ."

Paddington wasn't sure what happened next. His feet felt like lead as he tried to scramble out of the hole in order to escape, but try as he might he couldn't gain a foothold. Above it all was the loud buzzing of the probe, together with the sound of voices, and then . . .

"Paddington!" Mrs Brown's voice came to him through the haze. "Paddington! What *are* you doing? We wondered where on earth you'd got to."

"Fancy going to sleep in the garden at this time of the year," said Judy, shining her torch on him. "You'll catch your death of cold."

"And Dad won't be too pleased if you wear out his batteries," said Jonathan, reaching down to switch off the Magic-probe.

As the noise stopped Paddington stood up and

rubbed his eyes. "I think," he announced to the world in general, "I've been having a daymare. That's the same as a nightmare," he explained, "only much, *much* worse. Especially when it's about Mr Curry."

"Well," said Mrs Bird, "if the noise you were making and the way you were jumping about was anything to go by, I, for one, believe you."

"I was trying to climb out of Mr Curry's hole, Mrs Bird," said Paddington. "I'd been looking for buried treasure — only it suddenly disappeared."

"Treasure," said Mrs Bird sternly, "buried or otherwise, has a habit of doing just that. You don't often get something for nothing in this world. How-

ever," she took hold of Paddington's paw and led
him up the path towards the house, "be that as it
may, you woke just in time."

Paddington knew better than to ask questions,
but as they arrived in the kitchen and the Browns'
housekeeper opened the oven door he nearly fell
over backwards with surprise, for there in front of
him, moist and glistening and golden brown, was
an enormous cake.

"It's made of pecan nuts," said Judy, as she
helped Mrs Bird lift it from the oven. "Not only
that, but it's shaped just like a Blue Peter badge."

Paddington could hardly believe his eyes and
he pinched himself several times in order to make
sure he wasn't still dreaming. It really was uncanny
the way Mrs Bird "knew" about things.

"I happened to come across your cake bro-
chure," she explained, reading Paddington's
thoughts. "It looked too good to resist."

"And then a certain person who keeps an antique
shop not a million miles from here happened to
mention your Christmas present problem," added
Jonathan, "so we all got together."

Paddington sniffed the air happily. Good though
Auntie Mabel's Pecan Nut Specials undoubtedly
were, he was sure they wouldn't have stood a chance
in competition with Mrs Bird's, and were he to be
armed with one of his most sensitive probes, even

Arnold Prosper would have been hard put to locate anything more delicious. It certainly more than made up for all he'd been through with Mr Curry in his daymare.

He licked his lips. "I think," he announced, amid laughter, "I'd better take it to the Blue Peter studio myself. After all, it's a bit difficult cutting a cake for so many people and they may need some help!"

CHAPTER SEVEN

Paddington in the "Hot Seat"

Paddington sat up in bed, and after peering at his reflection in a glass of water, ran a comb carefully through his whiskers. Then he wrapped a scarf round his neck, broke the end off a bar of chocolate, and dipped it into a newly opened jar of his favourite marmalade. That completed, he absent-mindedly began stirring a mug of cocoa with the end of a felt-tipped pen while he peered at an important-looking envelope lying unopened on his breakfast tray.

It was Christmas morning, and he was suffering

from his usual attack of not knowing which of his many presents to test first.

One of the nice things about living with the Browns was that the opening of presents was made to go on for as long as possible. Apart from having mounds of parcels round the tree, Paddington was always allowed to hang a pillow-case at the foot of his bed, and when he woke he usually found he'd mysteriously acquired a small stockingful of goodies into the bargain as well.

This year had been no exception, and apart from the parcels he'd already opened there was this very special envelope. It bore the crest of the British Broadcasting Corporation, and across the back, in bold letters, were the words NOT TO BE OPENED UNTIL CHRISTMAS DAY!

Paddington had never received a Christmas present from the BBC before and he grew more and more excited as he tore open the envelope and a large card fell out.

His eyes grew larger and larger as he took in the wording, and soon the whole household was in an uproar as he hurried downstairs in order to tell the others.

"Gosh!" said Judy enviously, "an invitation to see Sage of Britain! It's a special early evening Boxing Day edition as well."

"What a nice way to round off Christmas," broke

in Mrs Brown.

"There's a message on the back of the card," exclaimed Jonathan. "It's from the Blue Peter office, and it looks like John's writing. 'Best wishes for Christmas! Hope to see you there.' Peter and Lesley have signed it as well!"

"I wonder how they knew Paddington likes quiz programmes?" remarked Mr Brown.

"They're the sort who leave no stone unturned when they want to find out something," said Mrs Bird mysteriously. "They must have made some enquiries."

The Browns' housekeeper approved of Blue Peter. Over the years they had been very kind to Paddington; apart from that it kept him quiet every Monday and Thursday afternoon when he sat glued to the screen while he followed the fortunes of the team.

However, undoubtedly the second favourite programme at number thirty-two Windsor Gardens was Sage of Britain.

Sage of Britain was a quiz show in which each contestant had two bites of the cherry as it were. First they had to answer questions on a subject of their choice, then they had to talk for a further three minutes on another subject. The one who got the most votes from viewers at the end of the series was pronounced the winner and awarded the title of

Chief Sage for the year.

Although Paddington liked quiz programmes, he'd never actually seen Sage of Britain as it usually came on after he'd gone to bed. However, when the others explained the rules he decided it sounded very good value indeed — especially the bit about having two bites of a cherry.

Paddington was up bright and early the next morning, and he spent most of the day poring over Mr Brown's encyclopaedias so that he could take full advantage of his outing.

"I do hope he'll be all right," said Mrs Brown anxiously as he set off in a taxi soon after tea. "I never like him going out by himself after it gets dark — especially on Boxing Day."

"Perhaps we shall see him on the screen," said Judy. "They often have shots of the audience."

"I shouldn't worry yourselves," said Mrs Bird. "I spoke to the Blue Peter office on the 'phone only the other day and they promised they would see him safely home. Besides, he knows enough people at the Television Centre."

In saying that Paddington knew lots of people at the BBC Mrs Bird was making something of an understatement. Through his many visits to the Blue Peter studio he'd become a familiar figure with the staff. The result was that as soon as he showed his head round the door of the entrance hall people started rushing up to greet him.

What with one thing and another, it wasn't until a few minutes before the programme was due to start that he suddenly realized the time, and he had to say some very rapid goodbyes indeed before hurrying off in search of the studio.

On the face of it the BBC Television Centre was a very simple building. It was shaped like a giant hollow cake, with all the studios radiating out from the bottom floor, joined to each other by layers of circular corridors.

The only trouble was that if you set off in the wrong direction you could easily end up with twice as far to go and it certainly took twice as long, which was why, when Paddington at last reached the right studio, he saw to his dismay that the red light was already on.

Pushing open the heavy soundproof door he found himself in a darkened area of the studio.

"Sorry, mate," said a stalwart commissionaire, barring his way. "I'm afraid you can't come in once the programme's started."

"I can't come in!" exclaimed Paddington. He looked most upset as he peered at the man through the gloom. "But I've got a special invitation *and* I've spent all day studying Mr Brown's encyclo-paedias!"

It was the commissionaire's turn to look bothered. "My mistake, sir," he hissed, touching his cap as a mark of respect. "I didn't realize who you were. Come this way at once — then I'll let the Producer know you're here."

Sage of Britain attracted many famous contes-tants to the portals of the BBC. Over the years some of the best brains in Britain had taken part, and as was so often the case, beauty didn't always go hand in hand with brains.

"All the same," whispered the commissionaire to a friend, as he ushered Paddington into a small room at the side of the studio, "I reckon he takes the cake. He couldn't have been in the front rank when inches were handed out."

"I expect all the goodness went into his brains," whispered his colleague. "Did you see all them whiskers? Probably some kind of professor. Very erudite if you ask me."

The second commissionaire wasn't the only one to have taken note of Paddington's appearance.

Once inside the room Paddington found himself confronted by a girl in blue striped overalls, who sat him down in front of a mirror. She picked up a comb and eyed his reflection doubtfully as she helped him off with his hat.

"Do you part your fur in the middle?" she asked.

"I *never* part with my fur," said Paddington firmly. "I've had it ever since I was born."

"I didn't mean that," said the girl hastily. "It's just that I've never made up a bear before and I'm not quite sure what to do.

"We normally put some powder on the fore-head," she explained, "but yours is a bit er ... um ..."

"My forehead's a bit er ... um?" exclaimed Paddington hotly. "But I washed it specially this morning."

"Oh dear," said the girl. She broke off as the door suddenly opened and two men wearing head-phones came into the room.

"Sorry about this," said the first man. "I didn't realize we had another candidate." He hung a small microphone round Paddington's neck and then bent down to speak into it. "One ... two ... three ... testing. Good ... now you try saying some-thing."

"Something," said Paddington dutifully.

"I didn't mean 'something'," said the man. "I meant 'anything'."

Paddington gave the man a hard stare. He rather wished he would make up his mind. "Anything," he said.

The engineer looked at him wearily and then decided to have one last try. "Tell us what you had for breakfast this morning," he suggested.

Paddington looked most surprised. "I had some

chocolate," he announced. "Then I had bacon and eggs, and two mugs of cocoa, and toast and marmalade, and some sausages Mrs Bird had left over from the Christmas Dinner . . ." He bent down and opened his suitcase. "I've still got one or two left if you're hungry."

The others exchanged glances. "Ask a silly question," said the first engineer. He listened to his headphones for a moment and then took a closer look at Paddington. "You may have to have your whiskers trimmed," he announced. "We're picking up a lot of crackles. These microphones are very sensitive, you know."

"So are my whiskers!" exclaimed Paddington hotly.

"Perhaps you could use the ends in a crystal set," broke in the second engineer jokingly. "You know — like they did with cats' whiskers in the old days."

Paddington jumped up in alarm. "Use the ends of my whiskers in a crystal set!" he exclaimed in alarm. "I don't think Aunt Lucy would like that!"

He was about to explain that he wouldn't like it very much either, but fortunately for all concerned there was yet another interruption as a harassed looking man wearing headphones and clutching a clip-board suddenly rushed into the room.

"Terribly sorry," he said, holding out his hand. "Ronnie's the name — call me Ron. I'm the studio manager. Didn't have your name on my list. No-body tells me *anything*! There's not a moment to lose — you're on next." And before Paddington had a chance to say anything more he found himself being propelled at high speed through a maze of cables and wires, round the back of some sets and past some cameras, to where the audience was sitting.

The studio manager paused in order to give the signal for some applause, then he pointed Paddington in the direction of a platform on which a single chair stood bathed in the harsh glare of a spotlight.

"Quick," he hissed, giving Paddington a push. "You're in the 'hot seat'!"

Paddington raised his hat to the audience several times and then hurried on to the platform. So much had happened in a short space of time he didn't know whether he was coming or going, but he didn't at all like the sound of the latest develop-ment, so he bent down in order to make sure the chair was safe to sit on.

"It's all right, Ron," he called, turning to wave at the studio manager. "I think it's cooled down now."

If Lionel Pear, the questionmaster, was taken aback by Paddington's sudden appearance he was much too experienced to show more than the merest flicker.

"Do take your duffle-coat off," he said, hurriedly sorting through some cards on his desk. "You may find it a trifle warm under the lights."

"I don't think I will, thank you, Mr Pear," said Paddington. "I shan't feel the benefit afterwards if I do. Mrs Bird wouldn't like that."

Lionel Pear took a closer look at Paddington. "All right," he said grudgingly, "but do you *have* to bring your suitcase with you?"

"Yes," said Paddington firmly.

Lionel Pear gave a defeated sigh.

"May I have my points, please?" said Paddington.

"Your *points*?" repeated the questionmaster in a daze. "What points?"

"Well, you asked me a question, Mr Pear," said Paddington, "and I got it right. You asked me if I had to have my suitcase with me and I do. I've got my sausages in it."

"Hear! Hear!" called a familiar voice in the audience.

"Certainly not," said Lionel Pear with a touch of petulance in his voice. "We haven't started yet." He took a deep breath and then turned and beamed at one of the other cameras. The programme had been going particularly smoothly until a moment ago, but now a nasty doubt had crept into his mind. That was one of the troubles about a "live" show — once you'd started there was no going back.

But if Lionel Pear was feeling anxious about the unusual turn of affairs, his viewing audience — or that part of it watching the "goings-on" from the safety of the dining-room at number thirty-two Windsor Gardens, was even more alarmed.

"What *is* that bear up to?" exclaimed Mrs Bird.

"I said we might see him on the screen," said Judy excitedly. "I didn't dream he'd actually be on the programme."

"Ssh!" broke in Jonathan. "They're about to start the questions."

"Are you sitting comfortably?" called the questionmaster, as Paddington climbed on to the chair and settled back.

"Yes, thank you, Mr Pear," said Paddington. He peered down at the microphone on his chest and gave it a hard blow. "Testing," he called in a loud voice. "One ... two ... three ... testing."

A look of pain crossed Lionel Pear's face. "I suppose you realize," he exclaimed, "that you nearly blew my eardrums out!"

Picking up a small object from the table, he put it back in his ear.

"I'm sorry, Mr Pear," said Paddington. "I didn't realize you were deaf."

"I am *not* deaf!" shouted Lionel Pear. "I wear this ear-piece so that the Director can speak to me. Now, as you know, I shall be awarding ten points for each question you get right. What is your special subject?"

"Marmalade sandwiches," said Paddington promptly.

"*Marmalade sandwiches*?" The questionmaster tapped his ear-piece to make sure it hadn't been damaged when it fell out. "But I don't have any questions on marmalade sandwiches," he said plaintively.

"You could ask me where I can get some," said Paddington.

Lionel Pear riffled desperately through some more cards on his desk. "Well," he said, playing for time, "where *can* you get some?"

"I don't know," replied Paddington. "I was hoping you would tell me, Mr Pear."

He looked hopefully at the scoreboard.

"Is anything the matter?" asked the question-master.

"I was wondering if I could have my points now," said Paddington. "You asked me what my subject was, and I got that right. Then you couldn't answer my question about the sandwiches, so that's another ten for me."

Lionel Pear removed a handkerchief from his breast pocket and dabbed nervously at his forehead. "You're sure you haven't any more questions?" he enquired.

"Perhaps," said Paddington hopefully, "I could have my cherry now, Mr Pear?"

Although he'd done very well over Christmas, the lights were beginning to make him feel hungry again, and he hadn't even had one bite at the famous cherry so far, let alone the chance of a second one.

"I can't stand it," groaned Mr Brown. "Only Paddington would expect to get a *real* cherry."

"He's done jolly well," said Judy. She pointed

to the television set where a picture of the score-board had now flashed on the screen. "He's got maximum points for the first half."

"I think it's because there weren't any questions," said Jonathan. "It's one of the rules — only they've never had to use it before."

The Browns turned their attention back to the set as Lionel Pear reappeared on the screen.

Obviously labouring under a great strain, Mr Pear had plunged into the second half and was questioning Paddington about television in general.

Taking a furtive glance at the studio clock he saw that there was still five minutes to go before the end of the programme. Never had the hands moved so slowly, and the way things were going five minutes might just as well have been five hours.

"Right," he said desperately, "you have three minutes to tell us what changes you would make if you were running the BBC."

Paddington settled back in his chair. He had very decided views on the subject and he felt it was much more up his street.

"To start with," he said, "I'd have lots more cookery programmes. I'd have a special series on marmalade and another one on cocoa."

"A series about cocoa?" repeated the question-master. "You can't have a whole series about cocoa."

"Mr Gruber's got lots of books about cocoa," said Paddington. "You could even send an expedition out to South America to show where it comes from. And then you could have another programme all about getting the stains out.

"And I would have special sports programmes. There's lot about football and cricket, but there's never anything about important things like throwing snowballs. It's not very easy to do it properly — especially with paws.

"Then I'd have a special series for bears ..."

"*Bears?*" Lionel Pear permitted himself a superior smile. "Don't you think that's something of a minority programme?"

"Not," said Paddington firmly, "if you happen to be a bear!"

"All very interesting," said Mr Pear hastily, as to his great relief he caught sight of the studio manager about to give the wind-up signal, "but scarcely practical. Who on earth would you get to look after all these programmes of yours?"

Paddington gave Lionel Pear a hard stare; one of his hardest ever. For someone who was supposed to be in charge of a quiz programme Mr Pear didn't seem to know very much.

"The Blue Peter team, of course," he announced. "They can do anything.

"I'd put Mr Noakes in charge of cookery — some

of his recipes are very good.

"Then I would put Miss Judd in charge of removing stains, and Mr Purves in charge of the
Bears' programme. He's very good with animals.

"In fact," he continued, making his final point,
"if *I* was in charge of programmes I would make
Blue Peter last twice as long and I'd have it on *every*
day."

Somewhere in the studio a suspiciously familiar
voice called out "Hear! Hear!" and there was a
burst of clapping which was rapidly taken up by the
rest of the audience. In fact, the applause went on
for so long Lionel Pear had great difficulty in making himself heard. In any case, though, his attention
was obviously taken up with other things as he
pressed home his ear-piece and concentrated on
some last-minute instructions coming from the
gallery.

"Good heavens!" he exclaimed. "Good gracious!
Really?"

When Mr Pear at last turned his attention back
to Paddington it was with a look of new respect on
his face.

"I'm afraid," he said, "that because this is an
extra holiday programme we can't count it as part
of our regular series, but I've just been given some
special instructions.

"It seems," he continued, "that you've jammed

our switchboard."

Paddington jumped to his feet in alarm. "I've jammed your switchboard!" he exclaimed. "But I haven't been anywhere near it!"

Lionel Pear raised his hand to quell the buzz of excitement which ran round the studio. "It's been jammed," he explained dramatically, as the programme reached its final few seconds, "by thousands of Blue Peter viewers! They've all been phoning in to congratulate you on the best programme ideas they've heard for a long time, and by popular request it's my pleasure to name you CHRISTMAS SAGE!"

Paddington nearly fell over backwards with surprise at the news. "Thank you *very* much, Mr Pear," he exclaimed.

He considered the matter for a moment. Then, as the final credits began to roll across the screen, he came to a decision and opening his suitcase he produced a strange looking object in silver foil. Unwrapping it, he held the contents up to the camera then proferred it to the questionmaster.

"This is some special plum pudding Mr Noakes showed how to make last week," he announced. "It's the kind of thing you would have *every* day if I was ever put in charge, and it's a very good way to finish off a programme, especially a Christmas one when you've just been made a Sage!"